Chapter One

1819

"But, Sophie, you cannot do this!"

"I can do what I like!" Sophie replied.

It was hard to imagine that anyone could be more beautiful!

With her golden curls, pink and white skin, and perfect features, Sophie Studley had sprung to fame the moment the Bucks and Dandies of St. James's had set eyes on her.

After one month in London she was proclaimed an "Incomparable" and after two months she was engaged to be married to Julius Verton, who on his uncle's death would become the Duke of Yelverton.

The engagement had been announced in *The Gazette* and wedding-presents had already begun to arrive at the house in Mayfair which Lady Studley had taken for the London Season.

But now, two weeks before her marriage, Sophie had declared that she intended running away with Lord Rothwyn.

"It will cause a tremendous scandal!" Lalitha protested. "Why must you do such a thing?"

The difference between the two girls, who were nearly the same age, was startling.

While Sophie was every man's ideal of beauty and looked like an English rose, Lalitha was pathetic.

An illness during the Winter had left her looking, as the servants described it, "all skin and bone."

Because of long hours spent sewing for her Stepmother with an inadequate supply of candles, her eyes were inflamed and swollen.

Her hair was so lank and lifeless that it appeared almost grey. It was swept back in an unbecoming fashion from her forehead, which seemed to be perpetually lined with an expression of anxiety.

1

The two girls were almost the same height, but while Sophie was the embodiment of health and the joy of living, Lalitha seemed only an insubstantial shadow and on the point of collapse.

"I should have thought," Sophie said in a hard voice in answer to Lalitha's protest, "that even to anyone as half-witted as you the reason is obvious."

Lalitha did not speak and she went on:

"Julius will, it is true, become a Duke—I would not have contemplated marrying him otherwise—but the question is, when?"

She made an expressive gesture with both hands.

"The Duke of Yelverton is not more than sixty," she went on. "He may last for another ten or fifteen years. By that time I shall be too old to enjoy my position as a Duchess."

"You will still be beautiful," Lalitha said.

Sophie turned to look at herself in the mirror.

There was a smile on her face as she contemplated her reflection.

There was no doubt that her expensive gown of pale blue crêpe with its fashionable boat-shaped neckline and deep bertha of real lace was extremely becoming.

What was more, tight lacing had returned to fashion. The new corsets from Paris made her waist seem tiny and this was accentuated by her full skirts elaborately ornamented with bunches of flowers and ruchings of tulle.

"Yes," she said slowly, "I shall still be beautiful, but I would wish above all things to be a Duchess at once so that I could go to the Opening of Parliament wearing a coronet and play my part in the Coronation."

She paused to add:

"That tiresome, mad old King must die soon!"

"Perhaps the Duke will not keep you waiting too long," Lalitha suggested in her soft, musical voice.

"I do not intend to wait for either a long or a short time," Sophie retorted. "I am running away with Lord Rothwyn tonight! It is all arranged."

"Do you really think that is wise?" Lalitha asked.

"He is very wealthy," Sophie replied, "one of the

richest men in England, and he has a friendship with
the Regent, which is something to which poor Julius
could never aspire."

"He is older than Mr. Verton," Lalitha said, "and of
course I have never seen him but I imagine he is somewhat awe-inspiring."

"You are right there," Sophie agreed. "He is dark,
rather sinister, and very cynical. It makes him immense-
ly attractive!"

"Does he love you?" Lalitha asked in a low voice.

"He adores me!" Sophie declared. "They both do,
but quite frankly, Lalitha, I think, weighing the two
men side by side, Lord Rothwyn is a better bet."

There was a moment's silence and then Lalitha said:

"I think what you should really consider, Sophie, is
with whom you would be the happier. That is what is
really . . . important in marriage."

"You have been reading again, and Mama will be
furious if she catches you at it!" Sophie retorted. "Love
is for books and for dairy-maids, not for Ladies of
Quality!"

"Can you really contemplate marriage without it?"
Lalitha asked.

"I can contemplate marriage with whoever gives me
the best advantages as a woman," Sophie retorted, "and
I am convinced Lord Rothwyn can do that. He is rich!
So very, very rich!"

She turned from the mirror to walk across the room
to where the doors of the wardrobe stood open.

It was filled with a delecatable array of gowns for
which none of the bills, Lalitha knew, had been met.

But they had been essential weapons which Sophie
must use to attract the attention of the *Beau Monde;* an
attention which had brought her to date three proposals
of marriage.

One was from Julius Verton, the future Duke of
Yelverton, the second unexpectedly and in the last week
from Lord Rothwyn.

The third, which Sophie had discounted immediately,
was from Sir Thomas Whernside, an elderly, dissolute,
hard-gambling Knight who, against all expectations of

his friends who considered him a confirmed bachelor, had been bowled over at the first sight of Sophie's beauty.

There had of course been other *Beaux,* but either they had not come up to scratch or else they were far too impecunious for Sophie to consider them of the least consequence.

When Julius Verton had proposed marriage it had seemed for the moment as if all her dreams had come true.

It had exceeded Sophie's wildest ambitions that she should become a Duchess, and yet while she had accepted Julius almost rapturously, there were various disadvantages to be considered.

The worst was that Julius Verton had little money.

He was given an allowance by his Uncle as heir-presumptive to the Dukedom.

It was not a vast sum and it would mean that he and Sophie could live no more than quietly and in comparative comfort until he inherited the Yelverton Estates, which were some distance from London.

But it would be impossible to keep up with the fast and wildly extravagent London Society which Sophie enjoyed and envied.

There was however no question of her refusing such an advantageous Social alliance.

Lady Studley had hurried the announcement to *The Gazette* and the wedding was planned to take place at St. George's, Hanover Square, before the Regent departed for Brighton.

Sophie's days were filled with fittings at the dressmakers, with acknowledging the presents which arrived daily at the house on Hill Street, and with receiving with complacency the congratulations and good wishes of their acquaintances.

Sophie and her mother had not been long enough in London to have acquired any friends.

Their home, as they explained to all who wished to listen, was in Norfolk, where the late Sir John Studley's ancestors had lived since Cromwellian times.

Studley might be a respected name in the country, but it was unknown to the *Beau Monde.* Sophie's personal success was therefore all the more gratifying, because she had nothing to recommend her apart from her lovely face.

Everything had appeared to run smoothly until quite unexpectedly Lord Rothwyn had appeared on the scene.

Sophie had encountered him at one of the many Balls to which she and Julius Verton were invited night after night.

He had been away from London and had therefore not been already astonished or bemused by the first impact of Sophie's beauty.

Standing under a glittering chandelier, the candlelight picking out the golden lights in her hair and revealing the milky whiteness of her skin, Sophie was able to make the strongest of men's heads swim as she smiled beguilingly at those around her.

"Who the devil is that?" she heard a voice ejaculate, and she had looked across the room to see a man, dark and sardonic, staring in her direction.

She had not been surprised, for she was used to men staggering when they saw her and being at first tongue-tied and then over-voluble with their compliments.

Adroitly she managed to turn and speak to a man on her left, thereby revealing her perfect profile.

"Who is the gentleman who has just come into the room?" she asked in a low voice.

The Buck to whom she spoke replied:

"That is Lord Rothwyn. Have you not met him?"

"I have never seen him before," Sophie answered.

"He is a strange, unpredictable fellow with a devil of a temper but rich as Croesus, and the Regent consults him on all his crazy building schemes."

"Well, if he approved the Pavilion at Brighton he must be mad!" Sophie exclaimed. "I heard somebody yesterday describe it as a Hindu nightmare!"

"That is certainly a good description!" the Buck replied. "But I see Rothwyn is determined to make your acquaintance."

It was obvious that Lord Rothwyn had asked to be introduced to Sophie and now a mutual acquaintance brought him across the room.

"Miss Studley," he said, "may I present Lord Roth-

wyn? I feel that two such distinguished ornaments of
Society should get to know each other."

Sophie's eyes were very blue and her smile very beguiling.

Lord Rothwyn bowed with an elegance she had
somehow not expected of him, and she curtsied grace-
fully, conscious that her eyes were held by his.

"I have been away from London, Miss Studley,"
Lord Rothwyn said in a deep voice, "and returned to
find it has been struck by a meteor so imbued with divine power that everything appears to be changed over-
night!"

It was the beginning of a whirlwind courtship so
ardent, so impetuous, and in a way so violent, that Sophie was intrigued.

Flowers, letters, and presents arrived it seemed almost every hour of the day.

Lord Rothwyn called to take Sophie driving in his
phaeton, to invite her and her mother to his box at the
Opera, to arrange a party at Rothwyn House.

This, Lalitha was told afterwards, exceeded in gran-
deur, luxury, and amusement any other party to which
Sophie had been invited.

"His Royal Highness was there!" Sophie said in an
elated tone, "and while he congratulated me on my engagement to Julius, I could see he realised that Lord
Rothwyn was also at my feet!"

"I imagine it would be difficult for anyone not to
realise it!" Lalitha answered.

"He adores me!" Sophie said complacently. "If he
had asked for my hand before Julius, I would have accepted him!"

And now suddenly, at what seemed to Lalitha the
eleventh hour, Sophie had decided to run away with
Lord Rothwyn.

"It will mean sacrificing my big wedding. I shall have
no bride's-maids, no Reception, and I will not be able
to wear my beautiful wedding-gown," she said wistfully,
"but His Lordship has promised me a huge Reception as
soon as we return from our honeymoon."

"Perhaps people will be . . . shocked that you have

. . . jilted Mr. Verton in such a cruel manner," Lalitha said hesitantly.

"That will not prevent them accepting an invitation to Rothwyn House," Sophie assured her. "They will realise quite well that the number of parties Julius will be able to give before he becomes the Duke will be infinitesimal."

"I still think you should marry the man to whom you have given your word," Lalitha said in a low voice.

"I am glad to say I have no conscience in such matters," Sophie replied. "At the same time I shall make His Lordship realise what a sacrifice I am making on his account."

"Does he think that you love him?" Lalitha asked.

"Of course he thinks so," Sophie replied. "I have naturally told His Lordship that I am running away with him only because I am head over heels in love and cannot live without him!"

Sophie laughed and it was not a pretty sound.

"I could love anyone as rich as Rothwyn," she said, "but I do regret the Ducal strawberry leaves which would have been so becoming to my gold hair."

She gave a little sigh. Then she said:

"Oh well, perhaps His Lordship will not live long. Then I shall be a rich widow and will be able to marry Julius when he is the Duke of Yelverton after all!"

"Sophie!" Lalitha exclaimed. "That is a most wicked and improper thing to say!"

"Why?" Sophie enquired. "After all, Elizabeth Gunning was no more beautiful than I am and she married two Dukes. They used to call her the 'Double Duchess'!"

Lalitha did not answer, as if she realised that nothing would change Sophie's mind.

She had sat down at the dressing-table, once again absorbed in the contemplation of her own reflection.

"I am not quite sure that this is the right gown for me in which to elope," she remarked. "But as it is still a little chilly at night I shall wear over it my blue velvet cloak trimmed with ermine."

"Is His Lordship calling here for you?" Lalitha asked.

"No, of course not!" Sophie answered. "He believes

that Mama knows nothing of our plans and would be annoyed and would put obstacles in our way."

She laughed.

"He does not know Mama!"

"Where are you meeting him?" Lalitha asked.

"Outside the Church of St. Alphage, which is just to the North of Grosvenor Square. It is small, dark, and rather poky, but appeals to His Lordship in that he thinks it a right setting for an elopement."

Sophie smiled scornfully and added:

"What is more important is that the Vicar can be bribed to keep his mouth shut, which is more than one can say of the more fashionable incumbents who are in league with the newspapers."

"And where are you going after you are married?"

Sophie shrugged her shoulders.

"Does it matter, as long as it is somewhere comfortable? I shall have the ring on my finger and I shall be Lady Rothwyn."

Again there was silence and then Lalitha asked hesitatingly:

"And what about . . . Mr. Verton?"

"I have written him a note and Mama has arranged that a groom shall deliver it to him just before I arrive at the Church. We thought it would look better and be more considerate if he were told before the ceremony actually takes place."

Sophie smiled.

"That of course is really rather a cheat, since Julius is staying with his grandmother in Wimbeldon and he will not receive my letter until long after I am married."

She added after a pause:

"But he will imagine that I have done the right thing, and it will be too late for him to arrive offering to fight a duel with His Lordship, which would be embarrassing to say the very least of it!"

"I am sorry for Mr. Verton," Lalitha said in a low voice. "He is deeply in love with you, Sophie."

"So he should be!" Sophie retorted. "But quite frankly, Lalitha, I have always found him unfledged and a bore!"

Lalitha was not surprised at Sophie's words.

She had known from the very beginning of the engagement that Sophie was not in the least interested in Mr. Verton as a man.

The notes of passion and adoration that he wrote her were left unopened.

Sophie would hardly glance at his flowers, and she invariably complained that his presents were either not good enough or not what she required.

And yet, Lalitha asked herself now, was Sophie really any fonder of Lord Rothwyn?

"What is the time?" Sophie asked from the dressing-table.

"Half after seven," Lalitha replied.

"Why have you not brought me something to eat?" Sophie asked. "You might realise I would be hungry by now."

"I will go and get you a meal at once!"

"Mind it is something palatable," Sophie admonished. "I shall need something sustaining for what I have to do this evening."

"At what time are you meeting His Lordship?" Lalitha asked as she moved toward the door.

"He will be at the Church at nine-thirty," Sophie replied, "and I intend to keep him waiting. It will be good for him to be a little apprehensive in case I cry off at the last moment."

She laughed and Lalitha went from the room.

As she shut the door Sophie called her back.

"You might as well send the groom now," she said. "It will take well over an hour to get to Wimbledon. The note is on my desk."

"I will find it," Lalitha answered.

Again she shut the door and went down the stairs.

She found the note addressed in Sophie's untidy, scrawling writing and stood looking at it for a moment.

She had the feeling that Sophie was doing something irrevocable that she might regret. Then she told herself that it was none of her business.

With the note in her hand she walked down the dark, narrow stairs which led to the basement.

There were few servants in the house and those there were were badly trained and often neglectful of their duties; for every penny that Lady Studley had, and a great deal she had not, had been expended on the rent of the house and on Sophie's clothes.

It had all been a deliberately baited trap to lure rich or important young men into marriage and it had succeeded.

The person who had suffered had been Lalitha.

While they were in the country, even after her father's death, there had been a number of old servants who had continued to work in the house because they had done so for years.

In London she had found herself being alternately cook, house-maid, lady's-maid, and errand-boy from first thing in the morning until last thing at night.

Her Step-mother had always hated her and after her father's death had made no pretence of treating her with anything except contempt.

In her own home and amongst the servants who had known Lalitha since she was a baby, Lady Studley had to a certain extent tempered her dislike with discretion.

In London these restrictions disappeared.

Lalitha became the slave, someone who could be forced to perform the most menial of tasks and punished viciously if she protested.

Sometimes Lalitha thought that her Step-mother was pushing her so hard that she hoped it would kill her and faced the fact that it was not unlikely.

Only she knew the truth; only she knew the secrets on which Lady Studley had built a new life for herself and her daughter, and her death would be a relief to them.

Then Lalitha told herself that such ideas were morbid and came to her mind merely because she had felt so weak since her illness.

She had been forced out of bed long before she knew it was wise for her to rise, simply because while she was in her bed-room she received no food.

On Lady Studley's instructions, what servants there were in the house made no attempt to wait on her.

After days of growing weaker because she had literally nothing to eat, Lalitha had forced herself downstairs in order to avoid dying of starvation.

"If you are well enough to eat you are well enough to work!" her Step-mother had told her, and she found herself back in the familiar routine of doing everything in the house which no-one else would do.

Walking along the cold, stone-flagged passage to the kitchen, Lalitha perceived automatically that it was dirty and needed scrubbing.

But there was no-one who could be ordered to clean it except herself and she hoped that her Step-mother would not notice.

She opened the door of the kitchen, which was a cheerless room, badly in need of decoration, with little light coming from the window high up in the wall but below pavement level.

The groom, who was also a Jack-of-all-trades, was sitting at the table drinking a glass of ale.

A slatternly woman with grey hair straggling from under a mob-cap was cooking something which smelt unpleasant over the stove.

She was an incompetent Irish immigrant who had been engaged only three days previously as the Employment Agency had no-one else who would accept the meagre wages offered by Lady Studley.

"Would you please take this note to the Dowager Duchess of Yelverton House?" Lalitha asked the groom. "It is, I believe, at the far end of Wimbledon Common."

"O'll go when O've afinished me ale," the groom answered in a surly tone.

He made no effort to rise and Lalitha realised that the servants always learnt very quickly that she was of no importance in the house-hold and warranted less consideration than they themselves received.

"Thank you," she answered quietly.

Turning to the cook, she said:

"Miss Studley would like something to eat."

"There ain't much," the cook replied. "I've got a stew 'ere for us, but it ain't ready yet."

"Then perhaps there are some eggs and she can have an omelette," Lalitha suggested.

"I can't stop wot I'm adoing," the woman replied.

"I will make it," Lalitha said.

She had expected to have to do so anyway.

After finding a pan, but having to clean it first, she cooked Sophie a mushroom omelette.

She put some pieces of toast in a rack, added a dish of butter to the tray, and finally a pot of hot coffee before she carried it upstairs.

The groom left grudgingly a few minutes before Lalitha went from the kitchen.

"It be too late for goin' all the way t'Wimbledon," he grumbled. "Can't it wait 'til tomorrer mornin'?"

"You know the answer to that!" Lalitha replied.

"Yeah—Oi knows," he replied, "but Oi don't fancy bein' outside London after dark with 'em footpads and 'ighwaymen about."

"It's little enough they'll get out of the likes of ye!" the cook said with a shriek of laughter. "Get on with ye, an' when ye gets back I'll have some supper waitin' for ye."

"Ye'd better!" he replied, "or Oi'll drag ye out o'bed t'cook it for me!"

As Lalitha went up the stairs from the basement carrying Sophie's try she wondered what her mother would have said if she'd heard the servants talking in such a manner in her presence.

Even to think of her mother brought tears to her eyes and resolutely she told herself to concentrate on what she was doing.

She was feeling very tired. There had been such a lot to do all day.

Besides cleaning most of the house and making the beds, there had been innumerable commands from Sophie to fetch this and to do that.

Her legs ached and she longed just for a moment to be able to sit down and rest.

This was a privilege seldom accorded to her until after everyone had retired for the night.

She opened the door of Sophie's bed-room and carried in the tray.

"You have been a long time!" Sophie said disagreeably.

"I am sorry," Lalitha replied, "but there was nothing ready and the stew which is being prepared does not smell very appetising."

"What have you brought me?" Sophie asked.

"I made you an omelette," Lalitha replied. "There was nothing else."

"I cannot think why you cannot order enough food so that there is some there when we want it," Sophie said. "You really are hopelessly incompetent!"

"The butcher we have been patronising will leave nothing more until we have paid his bill," Lalitha said apologetically, "and when the fish-man called this morning your mother was out and he would not even give us credit on a piece of cod."

"You always have a lot of glib excuses," Sophie said crossly. "Give me the omelette."

She ate it and Lalitha had the impression that she was longing to find fault, but actually found it delicious.

"Pour me out some coffee," she said sharply, but Lalitha was listening.

"I think there is someone at the front door," she said, "I heard the knocker. Jim has gone to Yelverton House with your note and I am sure the cook will not answer it."

"Then you had better condescend to do so," Sophie said in a sarcastic tone.

Lalitha went from the room and down the stairs again.

She opened the front door.

Outside was a liveried groom who handed her a note.

"For Miss Sophie Studley, Ma'am!"

"Thank you!" Lalitha said.

The groom, raising his hat, turned away and she shut the door.

Looking at the note Lalitha thought it must be another love-letter. They arrived for Sophie at all hours of the day.

Lifting the hem of her dress, she started up the stairs.

As she reached the landing there was a cry from the back room.

Lady Studley slept in a small bed-chamber on the first floor because she disliked stairs.

Sophie's bed-room was on the second floor, as were all the other bed-rooms.

Lalitha put the note on a table on the landing and

went along the short passage which led to her Step-
mother's room.

Lady Studley was standing by the bed, dressed for a
Reception that she was attending in half an hour's time.

She was a large woman who had been good-looking
in her youth, but her features had coarsened with mid-
dle-age and her figure had expanded.

It was hard to realise that she could be the mother
of the lovely Sophie, and yet she could look attractive
if she wished.

For Social occasions she also had an ingratiating
manner which made many people find her quite a pleasant companion.

Only those who lived with her knew how hard, how
parsimonious, and how cruel she could be.

She had a temper which she made no attempt to control unless it suited her and Lalitha saw now with a
little tremor of fear that she was in a rage.

"Come here, Lalitha!" she said as her Step-daughter
entered the room.

Timidly she did as she was told and Lady Studley
held out towards her a lace dress on which the bottom
flounce had been torn.

"I told you," she said, "the day before yesterday to
mend this."

"I know," Lalitha answered, "but honestly, I have
not had time, and I cannot do it at night. My eyes hurt
and it is impossible to see the delicate lace except in the
day-light."

"You are making excuses for incompetence and lazi-
ness as you always do!" Lady Studley said scathingly.

She looked at Lalitha, and as if the girl's appearance
made her lose her temper she suddenly stormed at her:

"You lazy little slut! You waste your time and my
money when you should be working. I have told you
not once but a thousand times I will not put up with it
and when I tell you to do a thing you will do it at once!"

She threw the lace dress on the floor at Lalitha's feet.

"Pick it up!" she shouted, "and in case you forget
what I am telling you I will teach you a lesson you will
not forget in a hurry!"

She walked across the room as she spoke to pick up a cane which was standing in one corner.

She came back with it in her hand and Lalitha, who had bent down to pick up the dress, realised what her Step-mother was about to do.

She tried to avoid the blow but it was too late. It caught her across the shoulders and as she gave a piteous cry her Step-mother hit her again and again, forcing her down on her knees, raining blow upon blow upon her.

Lalitha was wearing a dress that had once belonged to Sophie.

It was far too big for her, and when she had tried to alter it the only thing she could do was to lift it in the front so that it was decent but it still remained low at the back.

It had become even lower in the last week or so, as she had lost even more weight.

Now the cane was cutting into her bare flesh, drawing blood and re-opening wounds that remained from other beatings.

"Damn you!" Lady Studley cursed. "I will teach you your rightful place in this house-hold! I will teach you to obey me!"

After her first cry Lalitha said nothing.

The pain was so intense and the horror of what was happening, as it had done before, left her feeling as if she could not breathe.

She was almost fainting and yet the agony she was enduring prevented her from reaching unconsciousness.

Still the blows fell until as Lalitha felt a darkness sweeping over her mind, a darkness that seemed interspersed with red fire as each blow tortured her body, the door was suddenly flung open.

"Mama! Mama!"

Sophie's voice was so imperative, so shrill, that Lady Studley's arm was checked in mid-air.

"What do you think has happened?" Sophie asked.

"What is the matter? What have you heard?" Lady Studley asked.

Ignoring Lalitha's body sprawling on the floor, Sophie held out to her mother the note which Lalitha had left on the landing.

"The Duke of Yelverton is dying!" she exclaimed.

"Dying?" Lady Studley echoed. "How do you know?"

"Someone has written for Julius to explain that he has had to leave immediately for Hampshire and had no time to see me himself."

"Let me look," Lady Studley said, snatching the paper from her daughter's hand.

She walked across the room to hold it near one of the candles on the dressing-table.

She read aloud:

"Mr. Julius Verton has asked me to convey to you, Madam, his most sincere rerets that he cannot present himself as he intended at your house this evening.

"He has been called to the bedside of his Uncle, His Grace the Duke of Yelverton, and has proceeded with all speed to Hampshire. It is regretfully expected that His Grace will not last the night.

I remain, Madam, yours most respectfully,
                    Christopher Dewar."

"You see what it says, Mama? You see?" Sophie asked in a voice of triumph.

"Was there ever such a coil?" Lady Studley exclaimed. "And Lord Rothwyn will be waiting for you!"

"Yes, I know," Sophie replied, "but, Mama, I must be a Duchess!"

There was a cry in the words and Lady Studley answered soothingly:

"But of course you must! There is no question of your giving him up now."

"I shall have to tell Lord Rothwyn that I cannot marry him," Sophie said uncertainly, "and I know he will be angry."

"It is his own fault!" Lady Studley snapped. "He should not have persuaded you to run away with him in the first place."

"I cannot leave him waiting there," Sophie remarked.

Then she gave a sudden shrill cry.

"Mama!"

"What is it?" Lady Studley asked.

"My letter to Julius! I told Lalitha to send the groom with it!"

They both turned to look at Lalitha, who was raising herself painfully from the floor.

Her hair had come undone and was sprawling untidily over her bruised and bleeding shoulders.

Her face was ashen and her eyes were closed.

"Lalitha! What have you done with the note for Mr. Verton?" Lady Studley asked sharply.

There was a pause before Lalitha could answer, then it seemed as if she forced the words from between her lips as she replied:

"I gave it to the . . . groom and . . . he has left!"

"Left?" Sophie gave a shriek. "Someone must stop him!"

"It is all right," Lady Studley said soothingly. "Julius will not be at his grandmother's house as we expected."

"Why not?" Sophie asked.

"Because this note from Mr. Dewar, whoever he is, tells us that he has gone to Hampshire."

Sophie gave a sigh of relief.

"Yes, of course."

"What we must do," Lady Studley went on, "is to drive to the Dowager's house early tomorrow and collect your note. We can easily make the excuse that you have changed your mind about something you had said in it. Anyway you will be able to tear it up and forget that you ever wrote it."

"You are clever, Mama!" Sophie exclaimed.

"If I were not, you would not be where you are today," Lady Studley answered.

"And what about Lord Rothwyn?"

"Well, he must learn that you have changed your mind."

Lady Studley thought for a moment, then continued:

"You will not, of course, give him the real reason. You must just say that you have thought it over and that you now think it would be wrong to break what is really your word of honour and you must therefore keep your promise to Julius Verton."

"Yes, that sounds exactly the right thing to do," Sophie agreed. "Shall I write to him?"

"I think that is best," Lady Studley agreed.

Then she gave an exclamation.

"No! No! A note would be a mistake. Never put anything in writing! One can lie one's way out of most difficult situations, but not if it is written down in black and white."

"I am not going to speak to him," Sophie said in sudden alarm.

"Why not?" her mother enquired.

"Because quite frankly, Mama, he rather frightens me. I do not wish to get into an argument with him! Besides, he is very over-bearing. He might extort the truth from me. I find it difficult as it is to answer some of his questions."

"It does not seem to me that he was ever the right sort of husband for you," Lady Studley said. "Well, if you will not go, someone else will have to."

"Not you, Mama!" Sophie said quickly. "I have said over and over again to him how much you would disapprove of my running away."

She gave a little laugh.

"It made him all the keener."

"I am sure it did," Lady Studley agreed. "There is nothing like opposition to make a man aggressively masterful."

"Then how shall we tell him?" Sophie asked.

"Lalitha will have to do it," Lady Studley replied, "although God knows she will certainly make a mess of it."

Lalitha was now on her feet and although a little unsteady, was moving towards the door with the lace dress in her hand.

"Where are you going?" Lady Studley enquired.

Lalitha did not answer but stood, hesitating, her eyes focused on her Step-mother.

The tears she had shed while she was being beaten had run down her face and her swollen eyes were still full of them.

She was so pale that Sophie said in an irritated way:

"You had better give her something to drink, Mama. She looks as if she is going to die!"

"And a good thing if she did!" Lady Studley retaliated.

"Well, keep her alive until she has told Lord Rothwyn my news," Sophie remarked.

"She is nothing but a trouble and a nuisance!" Lady Studley said harshly.

She went to the washing-stand, on which stood a bottle of brandy from which she frequently imbibed.

She poured a little into a glass and held it out towards Lalitha.

"Drink this!" she said, "although it is too good to waste on such a scarecrow!"

"I will . . . be all . . . right."

"You will do as you are told without arguing about it," Lady Studley snapped, "unless you want another beating!"

With difficulty, moving as if every step was an effort, Lalitha crossed the room and took the glass.

Because she knew that they were waiting for her to do so she drank down the brandy and felt it searing its way through her body.

Although she hated the taste of it she knew that it had brought her a new strength and dispersed the darkness that seemed to be still hovering just above her head.

"Now listen, Lalitha, and if you make a mistake over this I will beat you until you are insensible!" Lady Studlay said vehemently.

"I am . . . listening," Lalitha murmured.

"You are to go to the Church of St. Alphage in the carriage which will ge arriving at nine-thirty. You will find Lord Rothwyn there and you will explain to him that Sophie is too honourable, has too fine a nature, not to keep her word of honour. She has therefore decided that, rather than break Mr. Verton's heart, she must marry him as arranged."

Lady Studley paused to ask:

"Is that clear?"

"Yes," Lalitha answered. "But please do . . . not make me . . . do it."

"I told you what would happen to you if you argue," Lady Studley said menacingly.

She picked up the cane, which she had put down when she'd poured out the brandy.

"No, Mama!" Sophie said quickly. "If you hit Lalitha any more she will collapse and then she will be quite useless. I will talk to her. The carriage will not be here for another hour."

"Very well," Lady Studley said grudgingly, as if she regretted not being able to beat Lalitha again.

As they spoke they heard a knock on the door below.

"That will be the carriage for me," Lady Studley said. "Had I better go to Lady Corey's as we had planned, or shall I stay at home, having heard the sad news of the Duke's imminent death?"

Sophie considered for a moment.

"I think actually, Mama, you should stay. If Julius learnt that you were at a party after he had written to me, he might think it unfeeling of you."

"Of course, I should have thought of that," Lady Studley agreed. "How stupid of me. I was still covering our tracks where Lord Rothwyn was concerned."

She laughed.

"Oh well, I shall have to stay at home and spend a boring evening here. But at least it will give me a chance to make plans for the future! Oh, dearest, I have always longed to see you in a Ducal Coronet!"

"Thank God I knew in time," Sophie said in heartfelt tones. "I would never have forgiven myself if I had gone away with Lord Rothwyn and then heard that Julius was a Duke."

"We have had a lucky escape!" Lady Studley exclaimed.

She looked at her daughter and said:

"Take off that gown. You do not want to spoil it. It is one of your best."

"I will put on a dressing-gown," Sophie said.

"Yes, do that," Lady Studley agreed, "and take that scarecrow with you! Her death's-head upsets me!"

"Well, at least she makes herself useful," Sophie answered. "There is no-one else we can send to Lord Rothwyn to tell him the bad news."

"He will think it bad too," Lady Studley chuckled. "If ever I saw a man who was infatuated, it is His Lordship."

"He will get over it," Sophie replied.

She walked from the room and Lalitha followed her. But Sophie reached the second floor some time before her half-sister could struggle up the stairs.

"Come on!" Sophie said impatiently when at last Lalitha entered the bed-room. "You know I cannot undo this gown myself."

Lalitha put down the lace dress she was carrying, then she said:

"Sophie, do not . . . make me do this. I have a . . . feeling that His Lordship will be very . . . angry. Angrier even than . . . your mother."

"Why do you not call her 'Mama'?" Sophie asked. "You have been told often enough."

"I . . . I mean . . . Mama."

"I am not surprised that she gets into a rage with you," Sophie said spitefully. "You are so stupid, Lalitha, and if Lord Rothwyn also gives you a beating, it is no more than you deserve!"

"I could not . . . stand any . . . more," Lalitha whispered.

"You have said that before," Sophie remarked.

She glanced at Lalitha's face and said a little more gently:

"Perhaps Mama was rather rough with you tonight. She is very strong and you are so thin, I wonder her cane does not break your bones!"

"They feel as if . . . they are . . . broken!" Lalitha said.

"They are not or you would not be able to walk," Sophie remarked practically.

"No, I suppose . . . not," Lalitha agreed, "but I . . . cannot face . . . Lord Rothwyn and his . . . anger."

"You have never met him," Sophie said, "so what do you know about his anger?"

Lalitha did not answer and she said more insistently:

"Tell me. You know something, I can see that."

"It is just a . . . book that I found here in the . . .

house. It is called *Legends of the Famous Families of England.*"

"It sounds interesting," Sophie said. "Why did you not show it to me?"

"You do not often read." Lalitha answered, "and I was also . . . afraid it might . . . upset you."

"Upset me?" Sophie asked. "Why should it upset me? What did it say?"

"It recounted the origins of the Rothwyn family and how the founder, Sir Hengist Rothwyn, was an adventurer and a pirate."

"Yes, go on," Sophie said.

"He was very successful and was also known to have been very fierce."

Lalitha saw that Sophie was listening and went on:

"All down the centuries, so this book said, the Roth-wyns have inherited the uncontrollable temper of their ancestor. Lord Rothwyn's name, 'Inigo,' means 'fiery.' "

"I think I am well rid of that particular gentleman!" Sophie remarked dryly.

"There was a verse about Sir Hengist written in 1540," Lalitha continued as if Sophie had not spoken.

"What did it say?" Sophie asked.

Lalitha thought for a moment.

Then in a weak voice which trembled as she spoke she recited:

> "Black eyes, black hair,
> Black anger, so beware,
> If revenge a Rothwyn swear!"

Sophie laughed.

"You do not think I am afraid of that balderdash!" she sneered.

Chapter Two

Driving towards the Church in the hired carriage which should have been carrying Sophie, Lalitha wished she did not feel so ill.

The brandy which her Step-mother had given her after the beating had made her feel better for a short time, but now a strange and an unnatural lassitude was sweeping over her and her back was beginning to throb unbearably.

She knew she should be grateful to Sophie for preventing her Step-mother from beating her insensible, as she had done on other occasions.

Only the previous week Lady Studley had come to her bed-room with some complaint which had aroused her anger and found Lalitha in her night-gown.

She had beaten her then until she had fallen unconscious to the floor and lain there for hours.

Eventually it had taken all her resolution and what remained of her strength to crawl into bed. But she had been so cold from lying for so long on the floor that she had been unable to sleep or to keep her teeth from chattering until it was time for her to rise.

She was sensible enough to realise that she was growing weaker and that her illness after Christmas had swept away almost the last resistance she had to her Step-mother's cruelty.

Often she had been so unhappy that she had wanted to pray to die, and then she thought of her mother and would not allow herself to show such cowardice.

Her mother, small, gentle, and fragile, had always admired people who were brave.

"We all of us have deeds of valour that we must do in our lives," she had said to Lalitha once, "but the hardest of them all do not demand physical bravery but rather mental and spiritual."

To let Lady Studley kill her, Lalitha thought, would be the coward's way out of the intolerable hell in which she found herself after her father's death.

Even after living for two years with her Step-mother she could hardly believe that the horrors that she experienced every day were not just part of a nightmare.

To look back on her childhood was to remember the happiness of years which seemed always to be filled with sunshine.

It was true that her mother was not strong and as the

years passed there was not enough money to do the things they wanted.

Neither of these had counted beside the inexpressible joy of being together.

Her father, a large, good-humoured, kindly man, had been both loved and respected by those who worked and lived on their Estate.

It was, Lalitha realised as she grew older, his kind disposition which kept him from being prosperous.

He could never bring himself to push a farmer for the rent he owed or to evict a tenant.

"I felt I had to give him another chance," he would say a little shamefacedly.

So there was never enough money for repairs, new implements, or for her mother and herself.

Her mother had not minded.

"I am so lucky," she would often say to Lalitha, "both in my husband and in my daughter. To me they are the most wonderful people in the world!"

Their days had always seemed full, although there had been few parties or Social events because their house, which had been in the Studley family for five generations, was in an isolated part of the country.

From a farming point of view the land was excellent, but their neighbours had been few and far between.

"When you are older you must go to London and enjoy the Balls, Assemblies, and Receptions that I found so entrancing when I was a girl," Lalitha's mother would say.

"I am perfectly happy to be here with you and Papa," Lalitha would reply.

"I suppose every mother wants her daughters to be Social success," her mother said a little wistfully, "and yet I had my London Season and came back to marry the man I had known since we were children together."

She smiled and added:

"But it was going out into the world, meeting the elegant and important men in London, which convinced me that your father was the only man I loved and with whom I wanted to spend the rest of my life."

"You were lucky, Mama," Lalitha said once, "your father's Estates marched with Papa's so you had a suitor on the door-step, so to speak. There is no-one here for me."

"That is true," her mother agreed, "and that is why we must save, Lalitha, every penny we can so that when you are seventeen and a half you can dazzle the *Beau Monde* with your pretty face."

"I shall never be as beautiful as you, Mama."

"You flatter me!" her mother protested.

"Papa says there has never been anyone as lovely as you, and I feel that is true."

"If you can convince me that you think the same when you return from London, I will believe you," her mother had replied.

But there had been no London Season for Lalitha.

Her mother had died one cold Winter unaccountably and without any warning.

For Lalitha, like her father, it was a disaster so tremendous and unexpected that it was difficult to believe that it had really happened.

One moment her mother was there laughing, looking after them, charming everyone with whom she came in contact.

The next moment there was only her grave in the Church-yard and the house was empty and still.

"How can it have happened?" Lalitha asked her father.

While he kept repeating over and over again:

"I did not even know she was ill."

But if her mother had died, Lalitha soon realised that her father had in effect died too.

Over-night he had changed from being good-humoured and happy to a man morose and churlish who sat drinking far into the night. He took no further interest in any of the things that had occupied him before.

She tried to rouse him from his lethargy but it was impossible.

One night in the Wintertime when he was driving home from an Inn where he had been drinking he had an accident.

He was not found until morning and by that time he was in a bad way.

He was brought back to the house and while he lingered on for over two months he was a man who no longer had the will to live.

It was then that Mrs. Clements came to the house ostensibly to help.

Lalitha could remember the previous year when her father had come back to luncheon one day and said to her mother:

"Do you recall a rather rat-faced individual called 'Clements'? He kept the Pharmacy in Norwich."

"Yes, of course I remember him," Lalitha's mother had replied. "I never cared for the man, although I believe he was clever."

"We patronised his shop," her father said, "because my father had always dealt there and his father before him."

"But Clements was not a Norfolk man," her mother smiled, "nevertheless he lived in Norwich for many years."

"I know that," Sir John replied, "which is why I feel I have to help his daughter."

"His daughter?" his wife asked. "I seem to remember there was some trouble . . ."

"There was," Sir John said. "She ran away when she was only seventeen with a young Army Officer. Old Clements was furious and said he would have nothing further to do with her."

"Yes, of course. I recall the incident now," Lady Studley said, "although I was only engaged to you at the time. My mother was deeply shocked at the thought of any young woman defying her parents in such a way, but then Mama was very strait-laced."

"She was indeed," Sir John said with a smile. "I do not believe she really approved of me."

"She grew very fond of you after we were married," Lady Studley corrected softly, "because she realised how happy I was."

Her eyes met her husband's with a look of perfect understanding and then Lalitha, who had been listening, asked:

"What happened to Mr. Clements' daughter?"

"That is what I have been trying to tell you," Sir

John answered. "She is back. I saw her this morning and she asked me if I could rent her a cottage."

"Oh, I am sure we do not want anyone like that on the Estate," Lalitha's mother said quickly.

"I was rather sorry for her," Sir John said. "The man she ran away with turned out to be an absolute blackguard. He never married her and left her destitute after a few years. She has been supporting herself and her child by working as a domestic servant."

"If Mr. Clements were alive the idea would give him a heart-attack!" Lady Studley said. "He always thought himself very superior. In fact he stood for Mayor at one time."

"Well, the Clements family will have nothing to do with the 'black sheep,' but I felt I could not turn her away."

"You have rented her a cottage?" his wife cried.

"The one near the Church," Sir John answered. "It is small, but large enough for a woman and a child."

"You are too soft-hearted, John," Lalitha's mother said. "She will not be received well in these parts."

"I do not suppose she will want to have any contact with village folk," Sir John answered. "She appears to be superior in every way. She is still a good-looking woman and her daughter is about the same age as Lalitha—perhaps a little older."

He paused and then said somewhat uncomfortably:

"She said if you were in need of help in the house she would be only too glad to oblige you."

"I am sure she would," Lalitha's mother said swiftly, "but we have everyone we need at the moment."

Lalitha had not seen Mrs. Clements, which was apparently what the new tenant called herself, until after her mother had died.

Then unexpectedly she had arrived and offered her services when things were most difficult.

Two of the older servants had retired, so they were short-handed.

Then there was an epidemic of fever that Winter and it was quite impossible for three of the remaining staff to keep their feet.

Sir John had not seemed to care.

He sat gloomy and unco-operative, drinking in his study or riding out to neighbouring Inns from which he returned invariably so drunk that he had to be helped up to bed.

Mrs. Clements had asked Lalitha if she could assist, and because she was so desperate the offer had been accepted.

She had proven to be a tower of strength keeping the house-hold going, and managing Sir John in a manner which aroused Lalitha's admiration.

It seemed as if only Mrs. Clements could persuade him to eat as well as drink.

It was Mrs. Clements who had the fire burning brightly in his study and his comfortable slippers waiting for him when he returned from riding.

It was Mrs. Clements who could persuade him to make a decision about the Estate when he would not listen to anyone else.

When Sir John was brought home dying after his accident it was only natural that Lalitha should turn to the older woman for help.

"I'll look after him, dear. Don't you worry," she had said.

Lalitha, white-faced and incoherent with tears, had been content to let her manage things her way.

Afterwards Lalitha used to think that she should have realised what was happening.

But Mrs. Clements, soft-voiced, sympathetic, and compassionate, would have deceived a far more astute and worldly person than sixteen-year-old Lalitha.

She moved into the house and her daughter came with her.

Sophie put herself out to be as charming to Lalitha as her mother was, and Lalitha found in the incredibly beautiful girl the companion of her own age she had never had.

Only sometimes she thought that Sophie was rather high-handed, borrowing her clothes and even taking away some small trifles such as gloves, scarves, and ribbons without asking her permission.

Then Lalitha told herself that she was being selfish. She had so much and Sophie had nothing.

It was after Sir John died, the funeral over and his friends gone, that Mrs. Clements showed herself in her true colours.

The house was very quiet and Lalitha, wandering round in her black dress, thought how utterly and completely alone she was now that both her father and mother were gone.

She realised that she must sit down and write to her mother's brother who had moved from Norfolk to Cornwall.

Many years previously he had bought an Estate for himself and had remained there even after his father had died.

Her mother had always planned that they would one day go and visit him.

"You will love Ambrose!" she told her daughter. "He is older than I, and I think it was he who taught me to love the country so much that I was never tempted by the Social whirl of London."

But somehow there had never seemed to be time or enough money to go to Cornwall and there had been no question of her Uncle coming to them.

He had not even attended her mother's funeral although he had sent a wreath and a long letter to her father telling him how deeply he regretted his sister's death.

"I must write to Uncle Ambrose now," Lalitha told herself. "Perhaps he will ask me to come and live with him."

She had actually sat down at her father's desk in the study and opened the blotter when Mrs. Clements came into the room.

"I want to talk to you, Lalitha," she said in a tone which had an authoritative note in it Lalitha had not noticed before.

She also used Lalitha's Christian name, something which her mother would have thought to be an impertinence.

"Of course, Mrs. Clements," Lalitha said. "What is it?"

"I wish you to know," Mrs. Clements replied, "that I was married to your father!"

For a moment Lalitha thought she could not have heard right.

"Married to Papa?" she exclaimed. "It is impossible!"

"We were married and I was his wife," Mrs. Clements said furiously. "From now on I am Lady Studley."

"But when were you married and at which Church?" Lalitha asked.

"If you know what is best for you you will not ask me too many question," Mrs. Clements replied. "You will accept the situation and realise you are my Step-daughter."

"I . . . I am afraid I do not . . . believe you," Lalitha said quietly. "I am writing to my Uncle Ambrose to suggest that I should go and stay with him in Cornwall. He cannot know of my father's death, otherwise I am certain he would have written to me."

"I forbid you to do so!"

"Forbid?" Lalitha exclaimed in astonishment.

"I am now your legal guardian," Mrs. Clements replied, "and you will obey me. You will not communicate with your Uncle or any of your relations. You will stay with me, and make no mistake, I am Mistress in this house!"

"But that is not right!" Lalitha protested. "Papa has always said that this would be my house if anything happened to him, and the Estate is mine too."

"I think you will have some difficulty in proving it," Mrs. Clements replied and there was something evil in her smile.

A strange Solicitor appeared, a man whom Lalitha had never seen before.

He produced a Will written in a shaky hand which might have been her father's after his accident, or might not.

He had left everything to "my beloved wife, Gladys Clements," and nothing to Lalitha.

She felt that there must be something wrong, but the Solicitor showed her the Will and assured her that it was not only completely legal but her father's wish.

There was nothing she could say to him and when he had gone she sat down and wrote to her Uncle as she had intended to do.

Mrs. Clements, or rather Lady Studley, as she now called herself, caught her going out of the house to take the letter to the post.

It was then that she beat her for the first time. Beat her until Lalitha cried for mercy and promised, because she had no alternative, that she would not write to her Uncle again.

It was perhaps because mentally, if unable to do so physically, Lalitha defied the woman who styled herself her Step-mother that she incurred her venom and spite.

The new Lady Studley was clever enough not to try to associate with the neighbours.

They learnt gradually of course that she had taken over the house and the Estate, and that she had married Sir John before he'd died. Few, if any, knew who she had been previously.

The name "Clements" was dropped as if it had never existed.

Nevertheless it gave Lalitha a shock when she realised that Sophie now called herself "Studley."

"You are not my sister!" Lalitha stormed at her, "and my father was not yours, so how can you bear my name?"

Sophie's mother had come into the room while Lalitha was speaking.

"Who says that your father was not Sophie's also?" she asked.

She spoke slowly and there was a look in her eyes as if an idea had suddenly come to her.

"You know he was not," Lalitha replied. "You only came here a year ago."

She realised that her Step-mother was not listening to her and for once she was not being punished for answering back.

For a year nothing more was said.

They kept very much to themselves, but Lalitha realised that Lady Studley was squeezing every penny she could out of the Estate.

There was no question now of farmers being late with their rent or impoverished tenants being allowed any grace.

The farms were sold off one by one; the cottages

went to whoever could find the price for them; the gardeners were dismissed. The flowers which had given her mother so much joy were choked with weeds.

Slowly too the more valuable things in the house disappeared.

First a pair of Queen Anne mirrors which had once hung in her mother's home were taken away to be repaired and were never returned.

Then the family portraits were sent to London to an Auction.

"You had no right to sell those," Lalitha had challenged her Step-mother. "They belong to the family. As Papa had no son, I would wish my son to have them."

"Are you so sure you will have one?" Lady Studley sneered. "Do you imagine anyone would marry you? Or that I could dispense with your valuable services?"

She spoke sarcastically; for by this time Lalitha had become nothing more nor less than an unpaid servant.

She thought with a little throb of horror that this might be her position for the rest of her life.

Sophie was eighteen the previous Summer and Lalitha was surprised that Lady Studley had made no attempt to take her to London or to entertain for her.

By now she was overwhelmingly beautiful and Lalitha thought, in all sincerity, that it would be impossible for any other girl to be as lovely.

It was after Christmas when she realised why there had been a delay.

"Sophie is seventeen and a half," Lady Studley said in January.

Lalitha looked at her in surprise, knowing full well that Sophie was eighteen.

But by now she had learnt not to contradict, nor to argue, unless she wished to be beaten violently for her impertinence.

"She was born," Lady Studley continued, "on the third day of May, on which day we will celebrate her birth-day."

"But that is my birth-day!" Lalitha exclaimed. "I shall be eighteen on the third of May."

"You have made a mistake," Lady Studley replied. "You were eighteen last year on the tenth of July."

"No! That was Sophie's birthday!" Lalitha said in bewilderment.

"Are you really prepared to argue with me?" Lady Studley asked.

There was an expression on her face which made Lalitha recoil from her.

"No . . . no," she said in a frightened tone.

"Sophie is my child and your father's," Lady Studley went on quietly. "She was born ten months after we were married and of course I can easily prove it. You are also my child and the child of your father, but unfortunately you were born out of wedlock!"

"What are you saying? I do not . . . understand!" Lalitha cried.

Lady Studley made it brutally clear.

She was to be Sophie and Sophie was to be she. Only as a concession her father was not an unknown Army Officer but Sir John.

"Do you suppose anyone will question what I say when we reach London?" Lady Studley had asked.

Lalitha could not answer. She knew no-one in London and who would believe her word against Lady Studley's?

She was defeated. There was nothing she could do and nothing she could say.

It was intolerable to think that this common, pushing woman was pretending to be her mother.

She had taken her mother's place and had appropriated every penny.

But there was no-one to whom she could turn; no-one she felt would listen to her story.

Beaten and knocked about by Lady Studley, she had no presence.

She did not even look, she told herself, like a lady anymore, but the slatternly love-child who Lady Studley told her was kept only out of charity.

She was also to call this usurper "Mama" as she had called her own mother.

If she forgot to do so Lady Studley beat her, and after a time it was almost impossible to go on fighting, even for her mother's memory.

Lady Studley planned her entrance into Society on

her arrival in London with a cleverness which Lalitha would have been bound to admire if she herself had not had to suffer in the process.

The money that she had raised was not going to last long; only long enough, as far as Lady Studley was concerned, for Sophie to make an important marriage.

For Lalitha there would not be a penny-piece and she had the feeling that once Lady Studley had achieved her ambition, she would be thrown into the gutter and they would wash their hands of her.

In the meantime she waited on them as a servant.

Sometimes she planned to write to her Uncle, but there were so many complications and such violent penalties if she were to be caught doing so.

Then three weeks after they arrived in London Lady Studley threw the newspaper at her with a coarse laugh.

"Your Uncle is dead," she said. "You can read about it in the Death Column!"

"Dead!" Lalitha cried.

"You will not be able to afford time to mourn him!" her Step-mother sneered. "So get on with your work!"

Lalitha knew then that her last hope of escape had gone. She found herself just existing from day to day.

When she had finished each of the innumerable tasks that were set for her she was too utterly exhausted to do anything but seek the oblivion of sleep.

Lately Lalitha had begun to feel that her brain was affected.

Lack of nourishment and continual beatings made her feel so stupid that it was hard not only to remember things that she had been told, but even at times to understand what people were saying.

Now she tried to recall what Lady Studley had told her to say to Lord Rothwyn.

Her mind seemed blank and all she could think of was the agony her back was causing her.

She could feel her dress sticking to the open wounds that had been left by her Step-mother's cane.

She knew that when she came to take it off it would

hurt excruciatingly and as she pulled the material away from the scars they would bleed again.

Under her dark cloak she unbuttoned the back of her dress as far as she dared.

No-one would see it and as soon as she had performed the errand on which she had been sent she would go back and bathe the parts which hurt the most.

"If only this were over and I need not tell His Lordship," she murmured to herself.

She had a wild idea of running away, but where could she run to?

She had no money and no-where to go and if she went back to the house without having confronted Lord Rothwyn, she knew only too well what would happen to her.

The carriage was drawing nearer to the Church of St. Alphage. She could now see the spire, then the lych-gate, and beyond it the grave-yard.

Her Step-mother had ordered the hired carriage from a place where she had an account and the men had been told to wait for her, which Lalitha knew was a concession.

She might have been told to walk home.

Now the horses were pulling up and she drew in her breath, trying frantically to think what she had to say as the carriages came to a stand-still.

She pulled the hood of her dark, well-worn cloak down over her face. It covered her completely and was made of a warm material.

She felt cold and shivery but she told herself it was not so much the air outside as the fact that she was frightened.

"There is nothing to frighten me," she thought, "I am not involved in this. I am only a . . . messenger."

Nevertheless she knew as she stepped out of the carriage and walked through the lych-gate that she was trembling.

It was very dark in the Church-yard although there was a lantern hanging on the Church porch.

The grave-stones stood sentinal-like and accusing, as if they were shocked at the lies she had to tell.

Hesitantly she moved down the path towards the porch, the Church looming dark and somehow ominous ahead of her.

Suddenly there came the sound of quick foot-steps, and before she had time to see who was approaching she felt strong arms go round her.

"My dearest, you have come! I knew you would!"

As she looked up to protest a man's mouth was on hers.

For a moment she was shocked into immobility.

It was impossible to move and insistent, passionate, demanding lips kept her speechless.

Vaguely, far away at the back of her mind, she thought that she had not known a kiss could be like this.

Then with a tremendous effort she struggled and was free.

"P-please . . . please," she stammered, "I am . . . not . . . S-Sophie!"

"So I perceive!"

She looked up at him. In the light from the lantern she could see that he was taller than she had expected.

He seemed dark and over-powering.

There was a cloak hanging from his shoulders and she thought he looked like a huge bat, and just as frightening.

"Who are you?" he asked sharply.

"I-I . . . am Sophie's . . . sister," Lalitha managed to gasp.

She could still feel the pressure of his lips on hers. Although he was no longer touching her she felt that it was as if she were still in his arms.

"Her sister?" he queried, "I did not know she had one."

Lalitha tried to collect her thoughts.

What had she been told to say?

"Where is Sophie?"

His voice was harsh and seemed to her menacing.

"I-I . . . came to . . . tell you, My Lord," Lalitha faltered, "that she . . . cannot come."

"Why not?"

His abrupt questions disconcerted her.

She was trying to remember the exact words which she was to speak to him.

"S-she feels, My Lord, that . . . she must . . . do the . . . honourable thing . . . and she . . . must not break her . . . promise to Mr. Verton."

"Must you mouth that poppycock?" he asked harshly. "What you are saying is that your sister has been told that the Duke of Yelverton is dying. That is the truth, is it not?"

"N-no . . . I . . . do! . . . No!" Lalitha and involuntarily.

"You lie!" he snarled, "You lie as your sister has lied to me. I believed her when she said she loved me. Could any man have made a greater fool of himself?"

There was so much contempt in his voice that Lalitha made a desperate attempt to save Sophie from his condemnation.

"I-It was not . . . like t-that," she stammered. "S-she was . . . trying . . . to keep her . . . promise that she had made . . before she . . . met you."

"Do you expect me to believe that nonsense?" Lord Rothwyn demanded angrily. "Do not add lie upon lie. Your sister has made a fool of me, as you well know, but then what woman could resist seeing herself as a Duchess?"

He almost spat the words and then he said furiously, his voice seeming to ring out in the Church-yard:

"Go back and tell your sister that she has taught me a lesson I shall never forget. What is more, I curse her even as I curse myself for trusting her."

"No . . . do not say . . . that," Lalitha begged. "It is . . . unlucky."

"What has luck to do with it?" he asked. "Your sister has not only lost me a bride, she has also cost me ten thousand guineas!"

Lalitha looked up at the dark silhouette he made against the faint light in the back-ground.

Because she was curious she could not help asking:

"How . . . how can she have . . . done that?"

"I wagered that amount of money in the belief that she was sincere and true; that she was not a snob as all other women are; that rank did not mean to her

more than affection, a title more than the love they pro-
fess so easily with their lips."

"It is . . . for some women," Lalitha said quickly before she could prevent herself.

He laughed harshly.

"If there are, I have yet to find one!"

"Perhaps you . . . will, one . . . day."

"Do you think I would bet on it?" he asked savagely.
Then he said:

"Go on! Go home! What are you waiting for?
Describe to your sister my rage, my frustration, and
of course my despair because she will not become my
wife!"

There was so much unbridled fury in his voice that
Lalitha found it difficult to move.

She felt as if he mesmerised her by the sheer force of
his emotion.

It seemed to flow out from him so that she was bemused to the point where she was unable to obey him.
Yet at the same time she longed to run away.

"Ten thousand guineas!" Lord Rothwyn repeated.

Almost as if he spoke to himself, but still in the
loud, angry tones with which he had addressed Lalitha,
he went on:

"I deserve it! How can I have been such a besotted
fool? So brainless, so infantile, as to think she could be
any different?"

As if his words to himself galvanished him once again
into an uncontrollable anger, he stormed at Lalitha:

"Get out of my sight! Tell your sister if I ever set
eyes on her again I will kill her! Do you hear me? I
will kill her!"

He was so frightening that Lalitha turned to run
from him, run away back to the lych-gate and to the
carriage which was waiting.

As she turned, her head seemed to spin and she had
to pause for a moment to steady herself.

Then as she took a step forward Lord Rothwyn said
in a voice that was quieter but still menacing:

"Wait a moment! If you are Sophie's sister then your
name is Studley!"

Lalitha looked round in surprise.

She could not imagine why he was interested.

He was waiting for her answer and after a moment she said hesitantly:

"Y-yes."

"I have an idea," he said, "that I might save my money and perhaps my pride. Why not? Why the devil not?"

He put out his hand and took hold of Lalitha's arm.

"You are coming with me."

She looked up at him nervously.

"But . . . where?" she asked.

"You will see," he answered.

His fingers were hard and painful and they bruised her arm even though it was covered by her cloak.

He pulled her down the path towards the Church porch.

"What is . . . happening? Where are you . . . taking me?" she asked in a sudden fear.

"You are going to marry me!" he replied. "One Miss Studley is doubtless very like another, and it would be a pity to keep the Parson waiting for nothing."

"You . . . cannot . . . mean what . . . you say!" Lalitha cried. "It is . . . mad!"

"You will learn that I always mean what I say," Lord Rothwyn replied harshly. "You will marry me, and that will at least teach your lying, deceitful sister that there are other women in the world besides her!"

"No-no . . . no!" Lalitha said again. "I . . . cannot . . . do such a thing!"

"You can and you will!" he said grimly.

They had reached the Church porch by now and she looked up.

In the light of the lantern she could see his face and thought he looked like the Devil.

Never had she seen a man so dark, so handsome, but at the same time obviously infuriated to the point where he had lost control of himself.

His eyes were narrow slits and there was a white line round his set lips.

He did not relinquish his hold of her arm but rather tightened it as he dragged her through the door and into the Church.

It was very quiet and their feet seemed to ring out as he pulled her down the aisle towards the Altar.

"No . . . no . . . you . . . c-cannot do . . . t-this!" Lalitha protested in a whisper because instinctively the atmosphere of the Church made it impossible for her to raise her voice.

There was no answer from Lord Rothwyn.

He merely escorted her forward nearer and nearer to where, at the Altar steps, a Priest was waiting.

Frantic, Lalitha tried to release herself from his hold but it was impossible.

He was to strong and she was too weak to struggle with any fervence.

"I . . . cannot . . . please . . . p-please . . . it is . . . w-wrong! It is . . . c-crazy. Please stop . . . please . . . p-please."

They had reached the Altar and Lalitha turned her eyes towards the Priest who was waiting for them.

She thought that perhaps she could appeal to him; tell him that something was wrong.

Then she saw he was a very old man with dead-white hair and a kind, wrinkled face.

He was almost blind and he peered at them as if it was difficult for him even to see that they were there.

Somehow the words of protest died on Lalitha's lips and she could not say them.

"Dearly beloved . . ." the old man began in a quavering voice.

"I must . . . stop him! I . . . must!" Lalitha told herself, but the words with which she would have broken in would not come to her lips.

She felt as if everything was slipping away from her and she could not quite bring it back into focus.

She was conscious of the heavy scent of lilies, with which the Chancel was decorated; of the lights flickering on the Altar; of the peace and silence of the Church itself.

"I will not say the . . . words which make me his . . . wife," she told herself. "I will wait until we . . . come to them and . . . then I will say . . . no!"

"Will you, Inigo Alexander, take this woman for your wedded wife?" she heard the old priest say.

He went on, the words soft and mesmeric, until Lord Rothwyn replied loudly in a voice that seemed to ring out in the Church:

"I will!"

He was still very angry, Lalitha thought with a quiver of fear.

The Clergy-man turned towards her. Then there was an interruption.

"What is your name?" Lord Rothwyn asked.

"Lalitha . . . but I . . . cannot . . ."

"Her name is Lalitha," Lord Rothwyn said to the Clergy-man, as if she had not spoken.

He nodded. Then to Lalitha in his gentle, tired old voice:

"Repeat after me—'I, Lalitha . . .'"

"I . . . c-cannot, no . . . I cannot!" she began in a whisper.

She felt the pressure of Lord Rothwyn's fingers tighten on her arm.

They were extremely painful and compelled her as her Step-mother compelled her by sheer force to do what she was told to do.

She felt flickering through her the same fear that she felt when she waited for a blow of the cane on her back.

Now almost without conscious thought and without the agreement of her brain she heard herself stammer:

"I, L-Lalitha . . . take . . . t-thee . . . I-Inigo . . . A-Alexander . . ."

They left the Church and were driving together through the darkness.

Not in the hired carriage in which Lalitha had arrived but in a luxurious vehicle with crested accoutrements of real silver and with a sable rug over her knees.

She did not speak but knew without words that Lord Rothwyn was still as angry as he had been before.

She could almost feel his fury bubbling within him.

She could feel it exuding from him like thunder to fill the carriage and frighten her with its intensity.

She tried to think of what the consequence for her would be for taking Sophie's place at the Altar.

Somehow she could not believe that it was true. Everything was still out of focus.

"What will . . . happen to me? What will I . . . do?" she asked, yet the question somehow had no poignancy.

She only felt frightened to the point where it was hard to breathe, and so exhausted that if she were to fall on the floor of the carriage she would lie there forever and never get up again.

The carriage drew up at one of the large, magnificent houses in Park Lane.

There was golden light coming through an open door. Servants in claret livery decorated with gold braid ran a red carpet over the steps and opened the door of the carriage.

Lalitha stepped out first and stood bewildered and frightened in the huge marble Hall in which there were life-sized gilded statues set in alcoves.

"Come this way!"

Again Lord Rothwyn had his hand on her arm and was leading her across the Hall and into a beautiful room. She recognised from the number of books which lined the walls that it was a Library.

There was a large flat desk in the centre of the room and he led her to it.

A footman hurriedly lit two candelabra on the desk although there was already light from the silver sconces which decorated the walls.

"Is there anything you require, M'Lord?" a Major-Domo asked respectfully.

"No. Leave us, but keep a groom. I have a note for him to deliver."

"Very good, M'Lord."

Lalitha heard the doors close and felt herself quiver.

She was seated at the desk. There was a huge blotter in front of her decorated with a gold coronet over an elaborate crest.

Lord Rothwyn opened it.

"You are now," he said, "going to write a letter to your sister."

He drew some writing-paper from a drawer, set it down on the blotter, and held out a big white quill pen.

Automatically Lalitha undid the clasp at the neck of her cloak and pushed the hood from her hair.

It was still difficult to move her arm so she eased the cloak back a little further and took the pen from him.

"Now write," he commanded.

Obediently, because there was nothing she could do about it, Lalitha bent forward and put her hand on the paper to steady it.

" 'My dear Sophie,' " he dictated in a hard bitter voice, and she wrote it down as he went on:

" 'I gave Lord Rothwyn your message, and as he deemed it a pity to waste the services of the Priest and the festivities he had arranged for you, I have taken your place and I am now his wife.

" 'You will, I am sure, be delighted to learn that any fears for the health of the Duke of Yelverton were unfounded, and His Grace is expected to continue to enjoy good health for many years to come!' "

Lalitha stopped.

She had reached the word "unfounded."

"How do you . . . know this?" she asked.

She stared at what she had written, then said in a low voice:

"His Grace . . . lives in . . . Hampshire."

Suddenly she looked up at Lord Rothwyn standing beside her.

"It was not . . . true! It was you who sent that . . . note to Sophie! The Duke is . . . not dying at all!"

"No, he is not dying!" Lord Rothwyn replied. "It was a test—a test that your sister failed."

"How could you have done such a thing?" Lalitha asked. "It was under-hand . . . cruel!"

"Cruel?" he repeated. "Do you think it was cruel to query a love that had been professed again and again; a love in which I believed, but which existed only in my own damn-fool imagination?"

Again he was speaking violently and Lalitha felt almost as if he blasted her.

"Go on, finish your letter," he ordered. "The groom is waiting."

"I—I . . . cannot . . . write . . . this," she said. "They . . . will . . . kill me. They will . . . kill me . . . for having . . . taken . . . part in it!"

There was sheer terror in her voice.

She threw down the pen and tried to stare at the words she had written as they danced before her eyes.

"I am . . . mad! Mad to have . . . let you . . . do this . . . to me!" she said, "and . . . I cannot . . . stand any more. . ."

She put her hands over her face as she spoke and her head went forward onto the writing-table.

As she moved her cloak fell from her shoulders and slipped onto the chair behind her.

"Come!" Lord Rothwyn said harshly. "This is not the moment for weakness. They will not kill you for taking part in this masquerade. That I promise you!"

"I—I should . . . not have . . . done it," Lalitha said.

There was a desperation in her voice which arrested the words he was about to speak.

Then he looked down at her and saw her back. He lifted one of the silver candelabra from the desk.

Held above Lalitha's head, its light revealed the bleeding scars and weals on her back.

Her dress was unbuttoned to the waist and he could see the marks from Lady Studley's cane crossing and re-crossing themselves.

Some were deep crimson, some were bleeding, and others were purple bruises so innumerable that there was little white flesh to be seen between them.

"My God!"

The exclamation seemed forced from between Lord Rothwyn's lips.

Then he asked in a tone very different from the one he had used before:

"Who has treated you like this? Who has made those marks on your back?"

Wearily Lalitha raised her face from between her hands.

"Who can have done this to you?" Lord Rothwyn repeated.

He seemed to demand an answer and hazily, because

her head was swimming and she could not think clearly, Lalitha answered:

"My . . . Step-mother!"

Then as the words were said she cried frantically:

"N-no . . . no . . . it was my . . . mother. I did not say it! It was a . . . mistake! I-it was . . . my . . . mother!"

Lord Rothwyn, holding the candelabrum in his hand, looked at her in astonishment.

Rising from the desk, Lalitha turned towards him piteously.

"I . . . I . . . did not . . . say it," she said. "I . . . swear I . . . did not . . . say it . . . and . . . I . . . cannot . . . stand any . . . more. . . . I . . . cannot! I . . . cannot!"

She looked at him wildly, as if afraid that he would not listen to her.

She made a desperate little gesture, then collapsed on the floor at his feet.

Chapter Three

Lord Rothwyn stared down at Lalitha's prostrate body, then crossed the room and pulled at the bell-cord.

As a footman answered the summons he lifted Lalitha in his arms and carried her past the flunkey, across the Hall, and up the stairs.

The footman hurried ahead of them and opened a door at the end of a wide corridor.

Lord Rothwyn carried Lalitha into the bed-room.

It was a large room over-looking the garden at the back of the house. Decorated with lilies, it was obviously the bridal bed-chamber.

As he walked towards the bed Lord Rothwyn said: "Fetch Nurse!"

"Nurse, M'Lord?" the flunkey asked in surprise.

"You heard what I said."

Lord Rothwyn laid Lalitha down very gently on the pillows, setting her on her side so that her bruised and bleeding back was not against the bed.

He took his arms from her and stood staring at her, his expression still as incredulous as it had been when he had first looked at the terrible weals and scars left by Lady Studley's cane.

By the light of the candles he could also see that her arms were bruised.

He realised that when he had dragged her up the aisle it must have hurt as well as frightened her.

Lalitha did not move and Lord Rothwyn was also motionless.

The door opened and an elderly woman entered.

She had a kind, lined face, grey hair, and was wearing the conventional grey dress and apron of a children's Nurse.

"You sent for me, M'Lord?"

Lord Rothwyn turned as if in relief.

"Come here, Nattie!"

She crossed the room to his side and, following the direction of his eye, looked down at Lalitha and the terrible marks on her back.

"Master Inigo!" she exclaimed, "who could have done such a thing?"

She looked up at him as she spoke.

"Not me, Nattie," he replied. "I would not treat a woman or an animal in such a fashion."

"Who could have been so bestial?" Nurse asked.

"A woman!" Lord Rothwyn said briefly.

"What are you going to do about it?"

"That is what I am asking you," Lord Rothwyn said.

The Nurse bent forward and pulled apart a little further the sides of Lalitha's gown.

Bleeding, burningly inflamed, purple and orange tipped, there hardly seemed to be an inch of her back that was not mutilated.

"She has collapsed!" Lord Rothwyn said, as if he felt an explanation was necessary, "but when she is conscious the pain will be intolerable."

"It will indeed," the Nurse replied. "We need Bay-oil."

"I will send at once to the Pharmacy," Lord Rothwyn said.

He spoke briskly, almost as if he was glad that there was something he could do.

"No Pharmacy is likely to have the oil from a Bay-tree," Nurse said.

"Then where can we obtain it?"

"From the Herb-Woman."

"What Herb-Woman?" Lord Rothwyn began, and then exclaimed: "I remember! She lives near Roth. My mother used to speak of her."

"That's right," Nurse agreed.

She looked down at Lalitha again and touched her hand as if to reassure herself that she was still living.

It was a very thin hand and the bones of the wrist stuck out pathetically.

"Who is she, M'Lord?" Nurse asked the question as if it had suddenly occurred to her.

There was a pause before Lord Rothwyn said abruptly:

"My wife!"

"You have married her?" Nurse exclaimed. "But I thought . . . we were told this evening that . . ."

"—I was bringing home a great beauty," Lord Rothwyn finished with a note of contempt in his voice. "I was, but instead I have brought you, Nattie, someone who needs your care and protection."

The Nurse bent forward to put her hand on Lalitha's forehead.

"I'll do my best, M'Lord," she said quietly, "but we will have to leave her in God's hands!"

Lalitha stirred and was conscious of feeling happy.

It was something which seemed to come to her from the past and she knew that she had been dreaming of her mother.

It was a dream that had been recurring again and again. Her mother had been there with her, holding her, giving her something to drink.

After she had drunk she had been able to slip back into a land of dreams where she was a child and there was nothing to frighten her.

"Mama!" she murmured.

She opened her eyes and thought that she must still be dreaming. She was in a room which she had never seen before and it was filled with sun-shine.

She could see the carved posts of the bed in which she was lying, a marble mantel-piece of exquisite design, and above it a picture of brilliant colours.

She shut her eyes.

It must all be part of her dream.

Then because she was curious she looked again, only to find that the mantel-piece and the picture were still there.

"If you are awake," a quiet voice said beside her, "I have something for you to drink."

Now Lalitha remembered that she had heard that voice before.

It had been a part of her dreams. She had obeyed it instinctively.

An arm was slipped gently behind her shoulders and her head was raised a little to drink from a glass that was held to her lips.

Again she recognised something that had been in her dreams—the sweetness of honey in a cool liquid which had quenched her thirst.

"Where . . . am . . . I?" she managed to say weakly as the glass was taken away.

As she spoke she looked up and saw the face of an elderly woman who was smiling at her.

"You are at Roth Park."

"Where?"

"We brought you here, M'Lady."

"But . . . why?" Lalitha tried to say, and then she remembered.

There had been the drive to the Church-yard, the strange, unaccountable feeling of her first kiss, then the terror of being dragged up the aisle and the words of the marriage-service.

She had been married!

She felt, for a moment, a shaft of fear strike through her. . . .

He had been angry, very angry, and she had been afraid. . . .

Then she had written a letter . . . a letter to Sophie! . . .

Had she sent it? What had happened?

She could remember crying out in sudden terror at
something that she had said; something that was wrong;
something that she had promised never to reveal.

It was beginning to come back to her, but there were
gaps . . . gaps that were part of her fear, which was why
she knew that she was afraid to remember them.

"I am going to order you some food," said the quiet
voice beside her. "You will feel better when you have
eaten."

Lalitha wanted to protest that she was not hungry.

The drink she had just had was delicious; she could
still feel the sweetness of it on her tongue and it had
invigorated her so that she was thinking more clearly.

She knew that the elderly woman rang the bell and
gave instructions to someone at the door.

Then she came back to the bed-side.

"Are you still wondering how you got here?" the
woman asked.

Lalitha looked at her and said:

"Am I . . . not in . . . London?"

"No, indeed," the elderly woman answered. "You are
on His Lordship's Estates in Hertfordshire."

"His . . . Lordship?"

The words made Lalitha quiver.

Now she remembered. It was Lord Rothwyn she had
married. The Nobleman whom Sophie had jilted at the
last moment.

The dark, angry, overwhelming man who had set a
trap for Sophie and who had frightened her into marriage.

"How could he have done such a thing?" she asked
herself. "What can Sophie have thought when she realised that she had been tricked?"

The question made her think of Lady Studley and
she trembled.

"Does . . . does my Step-mother . . . know where I
. . . am?" she asked in a voice that was little above a
whisper.

"I don't know," the elderly woman answered, "and you need not worry about her or anyone else. His Lordship is looking after you."

"He-he was . . . so angry," Lalitha said.

"He is not angry now," she was assured. "He just wishes for Your Ladyship to get well."

There was something comforting in knowing that he was no longer angry.

Lalitha shut her eyes and fell asleep.

When she opened them again there was food waiting for her.

She was still not hungry but to please the elderly woman she tried to eat a few mouthfuls and succeeded.

Then she slept again, drifting away into a dream-land where her mother was waiting for her and no fear existed.

It was the following morning before she really felt that the clouds had moved away from her head and she could think more clearly.

The room was even more beautiful than it had appeared at first glance.

The white and gold walls, the pink hangings which matched the carpet, the huge, gold-framed mirrors; the pictures and flowers, all were part of an ideal room she had sometimes imagined owning but which never before had she actually seen.

Now she learnt that the elderly woman who attended to her had been Lord Rothwyn's Nurse.

"A sweet little boy he was, and 'Nattie' was one of the first words he ever said. It's stuck to me ever since!"

She brought Lalitha some breakfast and set it down beside her on the big bed.

Lalitha stared at it, yet for a moment she did not see the fine Worcester china, the gleaming silver, and exquisitely embroidered cloth.

Instead she saw the food she had eaten having cooked it herself on the dirty, unscrubbed kitchen-table at the house on Hill Street.

What would her Step-mother be thinking of her now that she was not there?

What explanations had been given when she had not returned?

What would they say to her when she saw them again?

Because she was frightened by such questions she forced them to the back of her mind and tried to listen to what Nattie was saying to her.

"You've got to fatten yourself up, M'Lady! Already you have put on a little weight!"

Lalitha stared at her, her eyes wide.

"How could I . . . have . . ." she began, and then asked in a tense voice: "How long have I . . . been here?"

"Nearly three weeks."

Lalitha started in such amazement that the china on the tray rattled.

"It cannot be true! Three weeks! But why? How can it have . . . happened?"

"You have been ill," Nattie replied. "It's what the Physician described as 'exhaustion of the brain,' but we didn't pay much attention to him, although His Lordship insisted on consulting him."

She paused, and as if she realised that Lalitha was waiting for her to explain she went on:

"It's the Herb-Woman who has been treating you, M'Lady. You won't recognise your back when you see it in the mirror."

"The Herb-Woman?" Lalitha repeated, thinking to herself that she must be stupid as she still could not understand what had happened.

"Famous she is in these parts," Nattie went on, "and people come down from London for her to cure their complaints with her herbs. She won't allow anyone to use Doctors' medicines. A lot of rubbish, she calls them!"

"Is it herbs that you have been giving me to drink?" Lalitha asked. "Even though I was unconscious I somehow knew they were delicious!"

"Herbs and fruits from her garden," Nattie said, "and honey from her bees. She would not use anyone else's. Says they have special healing powers."

Lalitha was silent for a moment and then she said:

"You say I am . . . fatter?"

"A little," Nattie answered, "and it's an improvement."

She went to the dressing-table and picked up a small mirror with a gold frame surmounted by dancing angels.

She carried it across the room and held it in front of Lalitha so that she could see herself.

It was a very different reflection from the one she had last seen in her bed-room on Hill Street.

At that time the skin of her face had seemed taut over the prominent bones. Her eyes, red and inflamed, had been half closed, and her hair had fallen in lank strands to her shoulders.

Now her eyes seemed almost to fill her small face, and although the line of her chin was sharp, her skin was translucently clear and had a faint flush of colour.

Her hair seemed fuller and more buoyant with a slight wave. It was parted in the centre and fell on each side of her face.

"I look . . . different!" she said at last.

"You will look very different before I've finished with you!" Nattie promised. "But you will have to do as I say!"

Lalitha smiled.

She knew that half-bullying, half-affectionate note which every Nurse used to her charges.

It was just the way her own Nurse had spoken to her and it hid a tenderness which she had never received from anyone else.

She knew it was love, in some ways like the love she had received from her mother, and in another way different, because Nurse would never 'stand any nonsense.'

"I will do what . . . you tell me," she said. "I want to get . . . well."

Even as she spoke she wondered if that was really true.

If she were well, would there not be problems to face? And one problem was greater than all the others.

She did not even have to express it to herself; she just knew that the thought of him, large, frightening, and angry, was there, however much she might try to escape from it.

Nattie brought her a fresh night-gown, an elegant creation of soft lawn trimmed with lace, and brushed her hair.

Before she did so she rubbed into it a lotion which she said the Herb-Woman had given her.

"What is it?" Lalitha asked.

"Cinquefoil, or as we used to call it as children, 'Five-fingered grass,'" Nattie replied. "It is the herb of Jupiter."

"Does it really make the hair grow?" Lalitha enquired.

"Your hair has grown quite considerably since you have been ill," Nattie replied. "But then it always does when a body is unconscious."

"I never knew that!" Lalitha exclaimed.

"It's true!"

"How could I have been unconscious for so long?"

"You could have awakened after a time, but you would only have been confused and unhappy, so we kept Your Ladyship asleep."

"With herbs, of course!" Lalitha said with a smile.

"Sleep is the healing of the Lord," Nattie said, "but we assisted Him a little."

"What did the Herb-Woman give me for that?" Lalitha enquired curiously.

"I think it was privet, St. John's Wort, and white poppy," Nattie answered, "but you will have to ask her yourself. Although she does not always give her secrets away."

Nattie brushed Lalitha's hair until she felt that it was almost dancing around her shoulders; then, because so much attention had tired her, she slept again.

When she awoke it was afternoon.

Tea was brought in and tiny sandwiches, again exquisitely served. When she had finished it Nattie said:

"His Lordship would like to speak to you."

"His . . . Lordship?" Lalitha could hardly breathe the words.

Instinctively her hands went up to her breast, as if she would protect herself.

"He has been to see you every day," Nattie went on, "to watch your improvement."

She gave a little laugh.

"It was almost as if Your Ladyship were one of those buildings on which he spends so much of his time!"

Lalitha could not answer.

She was trembling.

How could she see Lord Rothwyn? What could she say to him?

A sudden thought came to her.

He would want to discuss the future and how he could be rid of her.

She hardly noticed that Nattie had brought from a drawer a wrap made of chiffon and trimmed with wide lace, which she put round her shoulders.

She tidied Lalitha's hair again and then patted the pillows behind her.

Then, as if she knew instinctively that he was approaching the door, she reached it even as he knocked.

"Come in, M'Lord."

She opened it for him and he walked in.

Lalitha held her breath.

She had somehow expected him to be in black, as he had been that night at the Church.

She remembered his flapping cape which had reminded her of the wings of a bat.

But instead he was wearing riding-clothes. A cutaway blue coat, high cravat, and white turn-overs to his polished boots made him vastly elegant and at the same time much less frightening.

It was a second before she could force herself to look at his face, to find that his expression was no longer that of a devil.

Instead she had to admit that he was the most handsome man she had ever seen. But he was still tall and overwhelming and he made her feel very small and insignificant.

She did in fact look very unsubstantial and fragile in the great bed with its canopy of carved angels and its embroidered curtains of pink velvet.

The afternoon sun-shine gave the room a golden glow but still Lalitha looked shadowy.

Lord Rothwyn told himself that he had never seen a woman with such strangely coloured hair.

It seemed almost grey, and her eyes were grey too. The deep, dark grey of a rough sea with a translucent light behind them.

"I am so glad to see you are better," Lord Rothwyn said in his deep voice.

He saw that Lalitha's hands with their long fingers were holding the chiffon wrap closely against her breasts, and while her lips were parted she was finding it impossible to answer him.

"You have caused Nattie and me a great deal of anxiety," he said as if he were giving her time to compose herself. "But now every day we can see an improvement. Soon you will feel well enough to come outside and inspect my gardens. They are very beautiful at this time of the year."

"I . . . I would like . . . that," Lalitha managed to say.

"Then you must do exactly as Nattie tells you," Lord Rothwyn said. "It is something I have been obliged to do all my life!"

He smiled and a faint smile in response touched Lalitha's lips.

Then, as she felt he was waiting for her to say more, she added:

"I . . . am . . . sorry!"

"There is nothing to be sorry about. It is I who should be apologising to you."

"I . . . should have . . . stopped you," Lalitha murmured. "I was thinking this . . . afternoon about what . . . happened. It was very wrong of me to let you . . . do it."

"You could not help yourself," he said, making no pretence that he did not know that she was talking of their wedding.

"It was . . . cowardly of . . . me," Lalitha said. "Mama would have been . . . ashamed of . . . me."

She spoke without thinking. Then he saw the fear come into her large eyes.

He walked to the bed and sat down on a chair, drawing it near to her.

"We are married, Lalitha," he said, "and therefore there should be no pretence and above all no lies between us. The night you collapsed because I forced you cruelly and with a desire for revenge to marry me, you told me first that your Step-mother, and then you changed it to your mother, had beaten you."

Lalitha's eyes dropped before his and her fingers twisted each other together agitatedly.

She did not speak and after a moment Lord Rothwyn said:

"Let me make this quite clear: no-one shall ever hurt you again while you are under my protection. You are my wife and everything that you have suffered in the past is over!"

She looked at him and he saw a sudden light come into her eyes, as if she believed what he had said.

Then she said in a low voice:

"But I cannot . . . stay with . . . you."

"Why not?"

"Because you do not . . . want me . . . and if you . . . send me . . . away, no-one will ever know that you . . . married me."

Lord Rothwyn's eyes were on her face, and then he said in a rather strange voice:

"Are you seriously suggesting, Lalitha, that you are prepared to hide away the fact that we are married? To vanish out of my life?"

"It would be quiet . . . easy to . . . do," she answered, "and the only . . . possible solution as far as . . . you are . . . concerned."

"Why should you think that?"

"Because I am . . . not the sort of . . . wife you should . . . have, and you did not . . . wish to . . . marry me."

"I forced you to marry me," he argued, "and we both know it was an act of revenge on your sister. At the same time it was a legal contract as well as a religious one. I married a 'Miss Studley.' "

Lalitha was still for a moment and then she asked:

"Did I save . . . you from losing the . . . ten-thousand-guinea wager?"

"You did," he answered, "but I refused to take the money when it was offered to me."

"Why?"

"I will tell you the truth," Lord Rothwyn replied,

"just as I hope I shall always hear the truth from you."

He sat back in the arm-chair at his ease and there was no harshness or enmity in his voice as he began:

"When your sister said she would run away with me I took into my confidence two of my closest friends, one of whom told me I was a fool."

"W-why?" Lalitha asked.

"He said that Sophie Studley was out to marry only for Social advancement, and that if she was prepared to jilt Julius Verton in my favour, it was merely because the Duke was likely to live for a long time, so I was a better bet."

Lalitha remembered Sophie saying very much the same thing and in the same words.

"Because I imagined myself in love," Lord Rothwyn went on, "I turned on him furiously for even suggesting such a thing. 'Sophie loves me for myself,' I asserted, like any callow youth."

Just for a moment there was a hint of contempt in his voice before he continued:

" 'Let us prove it,' my friend suggested, 'I will wager you ten thousand guineas that if she thought the Duke would die tomorrow, Miss Studley would hold to her engagement with Verton.'

"I laughed him to scorn because I was so sure that Sophie's protestations of love were real. To prove it we concocted between us a letter which we sent to your sister for her to receive before she set out to meet me in the Church-yard at St. Alphage."

"It was a cruel . . . test," Lalitha murmured.

"Cruel or not, it showed that I was indeed making a fool of myself and my friend was right."

"So he really won the wager!"

"In actual fact he did," Lord Rothwyn said, "but I remembered just as you were leaving me in the Church-yard that the actual wording of it had referred to 'Miss Studley,' not to 'Miss Sophie Studley.' "

"I understand!" Lalitha murmured. "And it was . . . honest not to take the money."

"I am glad my behaviour meets with your approval," Lord Rothwyn said with a faint smile.

"At the same time," Lalitha went on, "the . . . damage is done as far as . . . Your Lordship is . . . concerned."

"The damage?"

"You are . . . married to . . . me!"

"It is hardly the manner in which I would describe our union."

"You said we would not . . . pretend," Lalitha said. "Then let us speak . . . frankly. You loved Sophie because she is the most beautiful girl in England. No-one could be more lovely! I am therefore a wife you do not love and whom you cannot even admire! The best thing you can possibly do is to be . . . rid of me."

"I really believe you mean it," Lord Rothwyn said slowly.

"I am thinking of you," Lalitha said.

"And what about yourself?"

"I shall be all right," Lalitha answered, "if you will help me."

"In what way?"

"I was thinking if you could give me a little money . . . only a . . . little," she said hastily, "just enough to rent a cottage in the country . . . I could go where no-one has ever . . . heard of me and you need . . . never see me again."

She thought that he was looking critical and added:

"I have an old Nurse rather like Nattie. My Ste— my mother retired her when we left Norfolk and I know she is unhappy. She would look after me."

"What do you think this would cost?" Lord Rothwyn asked.

Lalitha looked at him uncomfortably and then looked away again.

"If it was not . . . too much," she said in a low voice, "I am sure we could manage quite well on . . . one hundred pounds a year."

"And for this large sum," he said, "you are prepared to go out of my life forever?"

"I would never speak to . . . anyone about what has happened," Lalitha promised, "and then you could marry . . . someone who would . . . love you as you loved them."

"Do you realise that I am a very wealthy man?" Lord Rothwyn asked.

"Sophie said you were," Lalitha answered.

"And knowing that, you still think that one hundred pounds a year would be enough recompense for your service to me?"

"I am not . . . extravagant."

"Then you are very unlike most young women of your age."

Lalitha gave him a faint smile.

"Happiness does not depend upon . . . money."

She thought of how happy she had been at home with her father and mother, who could not afford to be extravagant, but they had all three of them known a happiness that could never have been expressed in gold, however many millions of it there might have been.

Lord Rothwyn's voice broke in on her thoughts.

"Again let me say, Lalitha, you are very different from most young women."

"That is not really . . . a compliment," Lalitha said.

He was silent for a moment before he asked:

"Have you any other plans for the future?"

She turned towards him and now he saw that her eyes when she was moved or afraid were almost purple.

"Y-you . . . would not . . . tell my . . . Step-mother or . . . Sophie where . . . I had . . . gone? They might . . . find me and then . . ."

Lord Rothwyn sat up and bent forward.

Without thinking as she pleaded with him Lalitha had stretched out her hand towards him.

Now he covered it with his own.

"Do you really imagine," he asked, "that I would do anything which might force you to suffer again such bestial cruelty?"

He felt her fingers flutter in his as if he had captured a bird.

"I think," Lalitha said slowly, "my . . . Step-mother wanted me to . . . die. You could . . . tell her I was . . . dead?"

"But you are very much alive," Lord Rothwyn said firmly, "and although I am interested in your ideas, Lalitha, I have plans of my own."

"What are they?" she asked.

He released her hand and again sat back in the chair.

"Did Sophie ever tell you," he asked, "what is my main hobby?"

"No," Lalitha answered.

"I have been absorbed for some years now in restoring to their former glory ancient buildings that have been forgotten and neglected."

"That must be very interesting!"

"I find it so," Lord Rothwyn replied.

"I remember now," Lalitha said, "Sophie did tell me that the Regent consulted you about his building schemes."

"We have the same ideas on many things," Lord Rothwyn said. "I have advised His Royal Highness about his buildings in Regents Park and at Brighton. He often honours me by approving of a house I have reconstructed or renovated from what was often nothing more than a pile of rubble."

"I would love to see one," Lalitha said impulsively.

"And you shall," Lord Rothwyn promised. "Quite near here there is a house which was originally built for one of the Statesmen at the Court of Queen Elizabeth."

Lalitha's eyes were on his as she listened intently.

"It had fallen into a lamentable state of disrepair," he went on, "and the Great Hall where the Queen herself had often dined had become a stable. The timbers had been stolen or used for farm buildings, the carvings chipped away or employed for fire-wood. Today it is nearly complete."

There was a ring in his voice, Lalitha noticed, when he spoke of the house he had been restoring, and then he went on:

"I also discovered quite by chance near St. Albans, which was at one time a Roman town, a small Villa forgotten and over-grown in what is now a wood. I cleared away the trees, dug beneath the surface, and found exquisite mosaics, marble tiles, and pillars of almost unsurpassed beauty."

"How clever of you!" Lalitha exclaimed. "I do see it must be a tremendous satisfaction!"

"I pride myself," Lord Rothwyn continued, "on having an instinct where these things are concerned. The Regent says he feels the same when he sees a precious antique or a picture that needs restoring and knows that underneath the dirt of ages there is the work of a Master Artist."

"You are never mistaken?"

"Practically never!" Lord Rothwyn said. "That is why I know I am right about you!"

"About . . . me?"

"I feel you need quite a lot of restoration!" he said, smiling.

Lalitha thought for a moment and then she said:

"What you have found has been exceptionally fine or beautiful in the first place. Where I am concerned your restoration will only be to . . . me."

"You are very modest!" he said. "Do you resemble your father?"

"No, I am like my mother," Lalitha answered, "but only a poor reflection of her, just a few characteristics. She was very beautiful!"

She spoke without thinking and once again Lord Rothwyn saw the fear in her eyes and a sudden tremor go through her.

"Of . . . course," she said, not looking at him, "she has . . . altered a great deal as she has grown . . . older!"

"I thought we agreed," Lord Rothwyn answered, "that we would not lie to each other."

"I gave my . . . word," Lalitha answered, "and . . ."

She paused.

"What were the threats if you broke it?" he asked.

"S-She . . . really . . . will . . . kill me!" Lalitha murmured almost beneath her breath.

"That is something that will never happen," he said, "but because I do not wish you to be worried by anything you might say to me, because I want you to forget all the horrors of the past, I will not press you."

He saw a little light of gratitude in Lalitha's expression.

"I want you to think of nothing but getting well," he said, "and then you can walk in the garden with me, and when you are strong enough I want to drive you to see the Spa near St. Albans and the Elizabethan house before I find a tenant for it."

He rose to his feet.

"Promise me you will not worry about the future?"

"I will . . . try!" Lalitha answered.

"We will discuss it again when you are strong enough, but think now only that I shall be very disappointed by a restoration of a building called 'Lalitha' if it does not come up to my expectations!"

Lalitha gave him a little smile.

"Please do not expect too much."

"I am afraid I am a perfectionist," he answered.

He took her hand in his and raised it to his lips.

"Sleep well, Lalitha. I will come and see you again tomorrow."

He turned towards the door, then stopped as she said:

"Why are you here in the country? You should be in London. It is still the Season."

"Very nearly the end of it," he replied, "and I really cannot trust anyone but myself where my buildings are concerned."

He smiled at her and then he was gone from the room.

Lalitha leant back against the pillows.

Her heart was beating fast and yet she was no longer frightened, as she had been when he'd first entered.

'How kind he has been,' she thought, and yet she felt that she should have pressed him further to be rid of her.

He was obviously being gallant, but she was well aware what sort of impression she would make on his friends.

They had expected his wife to be Sophie, the beautiful, incomparable Sophie, with her golden hair, blue eyes, and perfect skin.

Lalitha knew without being told that while there must have been many women in Lord Rothwyn's life he probably never before offered marriage to any of them.

Sophie had said that he was one of the richest men in England, in which case every ambitious mother would have wanted him as a son-in-law.

Any girl would fancy living at Rothwyn House in Park Lane or being the Chatelaine of Roth Park.

Wearing the family jewels in which Lord Rothwyn's wife would bedeck herself, she could be Hostess to all the great personalities in the land from the Regent downwards.

Sophie had one qualification essential to such a position—a beauty that would strike anyone as soon as they saw her.

There might be others with blue-blood, a great dowry, or perhaps an engaging personality.

'I have none of those things!' Lalitha thought.

She turned her head against the pillows and shut her eyes.

She had to be practical, she thought. She had to be sensible.

For a little while until she was well she could stay here in the midst of a beauty which moved her in a manner that was inexpressible in words.

She had always loathed ugliness, just as she had always loathed dirt, cruelty, lies, and deceit, all of which had been part of the life she had been forced to live.

Now she had escaped!

Yet she must not deceive herself into thinking it could last forever.

Lord Rothwyn had been kind to her, but only because she was ill and because in his anger he had forced her to do as he wished.

'At the same time,' Lalitha thought, 'he must despise me for being so feeble! If I had protested loudly enough, if I had refused to take the marriage vows, he would not be in the position he is in now.'

She gave a little sigh.

'I must save him from himself!' she thought, 'and from me!'

It was two days later that Lalitha was well enough to go downstairs, and before that she had met the Herb-Woman.

She was not quite certain what she had expected.

Not a strange old crone who looked as though she

had been baked in the sun until her skin was like brass and her eyes were blue as forget-me-nots.

She had been brought to Roth Park in one of His Lordship's carriages and had been delighted to see how Lalitha's health had improved and how there seemed to be a little more fat covering her thin bones.

"You got a long way to go, my dear," she said with a broad Hertfordshire accent, "but you be on the right road and all you have to do now is to follow my instructions!"

She wagged her finger at Lalitha.

"No cheating now!"

There were herbs for Lalitha to take which intrigued her. She was to continue with the Bay-oil, which had healed her back and which was still necessary where there were scars.

There were soft creams that she was to rub over herself after she had bathed and which, she learnt, contained cowslips.

There was calamint to take, which Lalitha learnt was the herb of Mercury and was not only good for the skin but for all afflictions of the brain.

"You sound as if you thought I was mad!" she expostulated.

"You starved your brain as you starved your body!" the Herb-Woman answered. "It needs feeding for it to be as strong as it should be. Calamint will help you. I will leave you a bottle. Let me know when it is finished."

There were so many other things that Lalitha, afraid that she would forget her instructions when the old woman had gone, wrote them all down.

One thing which was easy for her to remember was that she was now to change the lotion for her hair to one made of peach-kernels.

"Boil them in vinegar," the Herb-Woman ordered Nattie. "Fortunately peaches are easy to come by at this time of the year. They make the hair grow even upon bald patches and give it a lustre and a shine as beautiful as the peach itself!"

She also brought Lalitha some of her special honey

and told her that she must eat the comb because that was as important as the honey itself.

"How did you learn all these things?" Lalitha asked.

"My father was a Herbalist and his father before him. My ancestor was Nicholas Culpeper."

"Who was he?"

"A very famous Astrologer-Physician," the Herb-Woman answered. "He was the first man in this country to set down his findings where herbs were concerned."

She smiled at Lalitha and added:

"A study which goes back into the very annals of time."

"Yes, I knew that," Lalitha said, "but I did not know there were books about herbs."

"Nicholas Culpeper," the Herb-Woman said, "devoted his life to the study of Astrology and Medicine."

"How fortunate that he wrote it down!" Lalitha exclaimed.

"During the Civil War he fought on the Parliamentary side and was wounded in the chest," the Herb-Woman explained. "He cured himself and he thought if he had died his secrets would have died with him."

"That would have been a terrible loss!"

"It would indeed! So while he treated innumerable patients in Spitalfields he still found time to describe the medicinal properties of herbs and the directions for his compounds in what he called his 'Complete Herbal.' "

"Please, one day could you let me see it?" Lalitha begged.

"Certainly," the Herb-Woman replied. "I will let you see it when you come to visit me, and as you are interested you can see the herbs growing, inspect those I have dried ready for Winter, and speak to my bees!"

"Speak to your bees?" Lalitha exclaimed in astonishment.

"They like those they heal to speak to them," the Herb-Woman said. "I talk to them, tell them what is happening, and explain to them what their magical honey has to do."

She added simply:

"They never fail me!"

It seemed to Lalitha as if every moment she was at Roth Park there were new things to see and to learn about.

When she dressed, with Nattie's help, the Nurse brought from the wardrobe a gown she had never seen before.

She had worried as to what she would wear when she went downstairs, aware that the dress she had worn to go to the Church would seem very out of place in the beauty and luxury of Roth Park.

The gown Nattie held out for her to see was very lovely.

It had the boat-shaped neckline which was so fashionable, and the huge sleeves which ended tightly at the wrist would hide the thinness of her arms.

The skirt was full and ornamented round the hem with soft ribbons which somehow bespoke the magic word "Paris."

"Is that for . . . me?" Lalitha asked, wide-eyed.

"His Lordship has had a number of gowns sent down from London," Nattie answered. "I burnt those rags you were wearing the night I first saw you."

Lalitha blushed.

"They were all I had," she murmured.

"Well, you have a great deal more now," Nattie said. "But I do not wish you to tire yourself by looking at them."

"Can I have just one look?" Lalitha begged.

Humouring her as if she were a child, Nattie opened the doors of the wardrobe and Lalitha saw that there were more than a dozen gowns of soft, muted colours very unlike the striking hues that had become Sophie's brilliant pink, white, and gold beauty.

"How did he know I would look best in the very soft shades like Mama?" Lalitha asked herself.

She thought that he must have a fantastic instinct for such things.

Certainly her dress of a soft shade of blue which reminded her of "love in a mist" flattered her slight body and seemed to accentuate the faint colour that had come into her face since she had taken the Herb-Woman's mixtures.

Nevertheless as she went down the stairs she felt apprehensive.

Supposing after all he had done for her Lord Rothwyn was disappointed?

A liveried footman led her acoss the Hall and opened the door to what Lalitha saw at a glance was not the Grand Salon she had rather dreaded but a much cosier, smaller room.

It was filled with flowers and decorated with brocade-panelled walls and pictures of children.

Standing in the window which opened into the garden was Lord Rothwyn.

He turned, stood for a second looking at her, and then smiled.

For the moment she was no longer frightened and she moved confidently towards him.

Chapter Four

Lalitha came down the stairs with a lilt in her step followed by a small black-and-white dog.

Every day she had been at Roth Park had been full of discovery and delight!

First she had been shown over the house that had been built in the reign of Charles II and added to by every succeeding generation of Rothwyns.

She could not imagine that anything so large and imposing could still have the warmth, atmosphere, and intimacy of a home.

There were treasures wherever she looked, fabulous pictures and tapestrys on the walls; furniture which successive owners had brought from France and Italy, all pieces which complemented each other in their fine craftmanship and made as a whole a pattern of beauty which enthralled her.

In fact she found herself thrilled by everything she

saw, and to have the history of such treasures explained
to her by Lord Rothwyn was a delight she had never
known.

Engraved in stone over the front door were the
words:

This house has been built by Inigo the first Lord Rothwyn not only with bricks and timbers but with his mind,
imagination, and heart. Erected in the year of Our Lord,
A.D. 1678.

"I can understand him saying that," Lalitha cried.

"So can I!" Lord Rothwyn agreed.

"Is that how . . . you build?"

"Yes."

There was a pause and Lalitha longed to ask if in
restoring her, as he had said he was doing, he gave her
his mind, imagination, and heart.

But she was too shy!

In any case the last was impossible where she was
concerned.

Then Lord Rothwyn took her into his enormous Library.

When she saw its beautiful painted ceiling and thou-
sands of books giving the walls a patch-work effect of
colour she had felt breathless with excitement.

"Would I . . . would I . . . be allowed to . . . read
some of these?" she asked, eagerly looking up at him.

With his hand he made a gesture which embraced the
room.

"They are all yours!"

"I can hardly believe it!" she said beneath her breath.
"I have felt these last years . . . starved because I was
not allowed to read."

"Books are not the only thing of which you were
starved," he said.

She blushed and then said anxiously:

"I am better! I am not as ugly as I was."

"You were never ugly," he answered in his deep
voice, "but you did look somewhat neglected."

"I am trying very hard to eat everything I should. I
drink literally gallons of milk!"

She wrinkled her nose.

"It is an effort, because I do not like milk."

"Neither do I," Lord Rothwyn confessed. "But Nattie always insisted on my finishing my mug, so you must do as she tells you."

Lalitha laughed.

"She is so kind and yet she is very firm."

"That is why I was so well brought up!"

He was speaking jokingly but Lalitha answered seriously:

"She is exceedingly proud of you. She thinks all the good qualities you have are due entirely to her."

"And so they are," Lord Rothwyn agreed loyally, "but what about the bad?"

He looked at Lalitha with a cynical smile on his lips as he spoke, and she knew that he was referring to his bad temper the night he had forced her to marry him.

"I think," she said slowly, "that perhaps you are rather too . . . proud of being like your famous ancestor."

"You mean Sir Hengist?" Lord Rothwyn asked. "What do you know about him?"

"I read about him," Lalitha answered, "and the verse that was written about his anger."

"So that is why you told me that to curse Sophie was unlucky. Did you mean it would be unlucky for her or unlucky for me?"

"For both of you," Lalitha answered, "because I believe anger or hatred can harm those who feel it."

"I see that I shall have to be careful when I am angry in front of you!" Lord Rothwyn said.

He noticed that Lalitha glanced at him a little nervously.

He realised that while she was undoubtedly much better in health and looked very different from the beaten, half-starved girl he had carried up the stairs the first night they had been married, beneath the surface she was still afraid.

She was like an animal who has been cruelly treated and from every raised hand expected a blow.

There were other things he thought that had contributed to Lalitha's new-found happiness; the chief one being that one of his dogs, a small King Charles Spaniel, had attached itself to her.

Lord Rothwyn had several Spaniels and white spotted Dalmatians which followed him wherever he went, moving towards him with wagging tails as soon as he entered the room, always alert in case he felt inclined to take them off for a walk.

The King Charles Spaniel had gone to Lalitha's side the first day she had come downstairs.

She had felt its cool nose against her hand and bent down to pat it.

"I see Royal is making you welcome!" Lord Rothwyn remarked.

"Why do you call him that?" Lalitha asked.

"He was named 'Royalist' because of his Royal patron," Lord Rothwyn answered, "but we shorten it to 'Royal.'"

"He is very sweet!" Lalitha said. "I once had a dog of my own which I loved . . . very deeply, but . . ."

She did not finish the sentence and Lord Rothwyn knew by the expression in her eyes that the dog had been taken away from her—just another of the miseries which she suffered after the woman she now called her "mother" had come into her life.

Lalitha did not realise it, but without questioning her, because he knew that to do so brought that terrible look of fear to her eyes, he was compiling a picture of what had happened in her life before he had met her.

She so often forgot the part that she had been forced to play.

"Before Mama died we read so many books together," she said, and did not realise that the sentence was of significance.

"There was a man in Norwich who grew roses like those," was another piece of the jig-saw which Lord Rothwyn was gradually fitting together.

This morning as she came down the stairs Lalitha was excited because His Lordship had promised her that if she felt well enough he would after luncheon drive her over to see the Elizabethan house he had renovated.

He showed her a sketch of the house as it had been

when he first found it, crumbling into disrepair, the holes in the roof mended with sacks.

The windows were stuffed with rags, the beautiful Elizabethan red bricks utilised for pig-houses or to replace those that had crumbled away from adjoining walls.

"That was how it was," Lord Rothwyn explained, "and here are the plans of what we visualised the house had been from what foundations remained."

"It is big!" Lalitha exclaimed.

"A lot of the houses round here," he said, "were built not only by the Noblemen of the time but by the Burghers of the City of London, who found it a convenient coach-drive when they wished to visit the country."

"But this house belonged to a Nobleman?"

"Yes," he answered, "he was a great Aristocrat and must have looked down his nose at my roistering, buccaneering ancestors!"

"I wonder if he knows that any insults Sir Hengist endured are now forgiven and forgotten by you?" Lalitha smiled.

"Let us hope he approves of what I have done," Lord Rothwyn said a little dryly. "There is however one thing that remains unfinished. Would you like to help me?"

"Could I do anything to help you?" Lalitha asked. "You know I would like to above all things."

"I was going to wait until you had seen the house," he said, "but I will give it to you now. You will find it a difficult task."

Lalitha wondered what it could be. Then Lord Rothwyn took from a drawer a silver box.

When he opened it she saw that it was filled with scraps of paper.

"What is that?" she asked.

"We found these in a secret cupboard behind some old panelling," Lord Rothwyn said. "They had been chewed by mice and I thought at first they might have been State papers."

"Oh, what a pity!" Lalitha cried.

"When I looked at them closely," Lord Rothwyn continued, "I found what I think is part of a poem. His-

tory relates that Lord Hadley, for that was the States-
man's name, also wrote sonnets."

Lalitha looked surprised and he explained.

"All the gentlemen of Queen Elizabeth's Court fancied themselves as romantics and therefore expressed
themselves in verse to Her Majesty or to the lady of
their fancy."

He laughed.

"Most of their efforts were certainly not great liter-
ature but doubtless they gave pleasure at the time."

"Especially to the person to whom they were addressed," Lalitha said.

As she spoke she thought a little wistfully how much
she would like someone to write a poem for her, then
thought that it was never likely to happen.

"What I want you to do," Lord Rothwyn went on, "is
to try to piece these fragments together. Too much may
have been destroyed for you to be able to make any
sense out of them, but it would be interesting to see
what he wrote."

"May I really do that?" Lalitha asked. "I am very
proud and honoured that you should entrust me with
anything so precious."

"You are not to tire yourself," he said. "If you feel
your eye are beginning to hurt you are to stop at once!"

He paused and added:

"They are very different from when I first saw them."

"I had been sewing late every night and I had only
one candle," Lalitha explained. "When Nattie allows
me to do so, I will embroider your monogram on your
handkerchiefs. I am quite skillful at it."

Even as she spoke she wondered if she would be with
him long enough. Then her doubts were swept away
when he replied:

"I too should be honoured, but you will not attempt
it until you are quite well. Do you promise me?"

"I promise," Lalitha answered, "but you and Nattie
are spoiling me. I shall get fat and lazy, and quite useless for anything except lying about on silk cushions."

"That is what I would like to see you doing," Lord
Rothwyn said.

She glanced up at him.

As his eyes met hers she felt a sudden breathlessness and a constriction in her throat which she could not explain even to herself.

Then he looked away and put the silver box into her hand.

"I shall be waiting patiently to see what Lord Hadley wrote to some Elizabethan beauty," he said.

Lalitha was consumed with curiosity to see what she would discover and this morning she had wished to sit down at the table in her bed-room, but Nattie had shooed her downstairs.

"It's a lovely day, M'Lady. You go out in the sunshine and keep such tasks for a rainy day. Besides, I expect His Lordship will be waiting for you."

This was enough to galvanise Lalitha into hurrying.

She had put on a new dress of very pale orchid pink. It was a colour she had never worn before and she was wondering a little shyly what Lord Rothwyn would think of it.

"I am just like one of the houses he is re-building," she thought. "As he chooses the right carpets and curtains for the rooms, so he chooses my gowns."

There was something impersonal about the idea and yet it was a pleasure she could hardly express to herself to know that anyone, especially Lord Rothwyn, was interested enough to expend time and thought upon her.

She reached the Hall and turned to walk down one of the corridors which led to Lord Rothwyn's Study, where she was sure he would be at this time of the morning.

It was a room some distance from the State apartments where he dealt with Estate matters and where the plans and sketches of his buildings were kept.

Lalitha had nearly reached the door when it opened and a young man came out.

He shut the door behind him to stand for a moment in the passage staring blindly ahead of him before he put his hands up to his face.

Then crossing to the opposite wall, he stood supporting himself against it as if otherwise he might collapse.

Lalitha thought he was ill and moved quickly towards him.

Then to her surprise and horror she realised that he was crying.

For a moment she did not know what to do but because he evoked her pity she asked in a low voice:

"Can I help you?"

"No-one can—help me!" he answered through his tears.

There was something pathetic and at the same time disturbing at seeing a man cry.

"What has happened?" Lalitha asked.

"It was my fault," he answered. "I thought it was—wrong but I was too—frightened to say so."

There was an open door near to where they were standing and through it Lalitha could see an empty Sitting-Room.

"Come in here," she said gently, and taking the young man by the arm, his face still covered by his hands, she led him into the room.

"Tell me what has happened?" she asked.

He took his hands from his face and drawing a linen handkerchief from his pocket wiped his eyes.

"I am ashamed of myself, Ma'am," he said. "Please forget that you have seen me."

"There is no reason for me to do that," Lalitha answered. "I wish to help you, if I can."

"But I have already said," he replied in a choked voice, "no-one can help."

"What have you done?"

"His Lordship is incensed with me and no wonder."

Lalitha knew that she had been expecting this answer.

"Why is His Lordship angry?"

There was a pause before the young man replied:

"I have built one of the buttresses in the wrong position. I misread the plans. Whilst I felt it was not quite right I was afraid that His Lordship might be annoyed if I questioned him."

"And now he has discovered what you have done?" Lalitha asked.

"He has dismissed me."

The tears came to his eyes again but he wiped them away fiercely.

"I was so proud, so overwhelmed with gratitude, at being given the chance to work for him and I wanted to please. I tried. God knows I tried, but I was afraid of failing—so I failed!"

"I can understand that," Lalitha murmured.

She stood thinking for a moment and then she said:

"Will you wait here for me? Promise me you will not leave until I return."

As if he suddenly realised the unconventional manner in which he was behaving, the young man rose to his feet.

"Forgive me, Ma'am. I should not have worried you with all this, but now you have been kind I will leave, I hope with—more dignity!"

"No," Lalitha answered, "I am asking you to wait here until I return. Have I your promise?"

"If it pleases you," he replied, "although I do not understand . . ."

"Just wait!" Lalitha said.

She turned and went from the room closing the door behind her. Then, drawing a deep breath, she crossed the corridor to open the door to the Study.

As she had expected, Lord Rothwyn was alone.

He was sitting at his big, leather-topped desk and there were a number of plans spread out in front of him.

With a sinking of her heart Lalitha saw that he was scowling and angry.

She had not seen that look on his face since the night they were married.

Then as she stood in the doorway, her grey eyes wide in her small face, Lord Rothwyn looked up.

"Oh, it is you, Lalitha!" he exclaimed.

The scowl on his face lightened and he rose slowly to his feet.

Lalitha shut the door behind her and walked to the desk.

She stood in front of him without speaking. After a moment he realised that she was twisting her fingers together and said sharply:

"What has upset you?"

"I have . . . something to say," Lalitha answered, "but I do not . . . wish you to think it . . . impertinent."

There was a little tremor in her voice.

"Nothing you could say to me, Lalitha, would ever be impertinent," Lord Rothwyn answered. "Will you not sit down?"

He noticed that Lalitha sat on the very edge of a chair and he seated himself at his desk.

"I am waiting," he said, his tone gentle.

"As you . . . know," Lalitha began, "I am a . . . coward and frightened of so many things. When one is frightened one often does what is . . . wrong simply because . . . one is numb or stupefied by . . . fear."

Lord Rothwyn was still and then he said:

"I imagine that you have been talking to young Jameson, whom I have just dismissed."

"I know what he is . . . feeling." Lalitha said, "because Your Lordship is very . . . intimidating."

"Are you blaming me for this young man's incompetence?"

He seemed to be waiting for an answer, and after a moment Lalitha said in a very small voice:

"He was . . . afraid to . . . argue with you, as . . . I was."

There was silence and then Lord Rothwyn said:

"Are you not being rather brave in telling me this?"

"I am . . . sorry for him," Lalitha explained, "because when people are strong and self-confident they do not understand how . . . weak and . . . stupid others like . . . myself can be."

"Do you really think that is an excuse for bad workmanship?"

"I thought in this case it was an error of judgment," Lalitha said. "Everyone . . . whoever they may be . . . can make a mistake!"

A faint smile twisted Lord Rothwyn's lips.

"As I made one," he said. "All right, Lalitha, I am saying it for you. That is what you are thinking, is it not?"

She looked down. Her eye-lashes which had grown

thick and long since her illness were dark against her cheeks.

"I told you that . . . you might . . . deem it an . . . impertinence!" she said hardly above a whisper.

"I think perhaps you are not as fearful as you think you are," he said, "but as I have no wish to upset you, Lalitha, I will speak to Jameson. Where is he?"

Lalitha's eyes were raised to his and he saw a sudden light in them.

"In the room opposite."

"Stay here!"

He went out, closing the door behind him, and Lalitha found herself praying in her heart that he would be kind to the young man.

No-one understood, she thought, the horrible, insidious, snake-like fear which could run through one's body, sapping one's will to the point when one behaved foolishly simply because one could not think clearly.

Even now, she thought, she could hardly believe that she would wake in the morning without having to anticipate receiving blows and abuse all through the day.

She remembered how she was always alert, listening for the sound of her Step-mother's voice, feeling a sudden sickness inside her at the thought that she might have done something wrong and would be punished for it.

She had never been free of the terror which was with her waking or sleeping. She could never escape from the physical shrinking from the pain that might be afflicted upon her.

Lord Rothwyn came into the room and she looked at him apprehensively.

He did not speak until he had sat down again at his desk, and then he said:

"I have re-instated him. Does that please you?"

Lalitha's eyes lit up and she clasped her hands together.

"Have you really done that? Oh, I am glad!"

"I told you that I expect perfection," Lord Rothwyn said.

"Yes, I know," Lalitha answered, "but I think you

also expect beauty, and beauty, like Cleopatra's nose, is not always architecturally symmetrical."

"That is true!" Lord Rothwyn agreed.

"And . . . happiness," Lalitha said hesitatingly, "is . . . something of which one cannot make an . . . exact plan."

Lord Rothwyn lay back in his chair and laughed.

"I can see you are going to upset all the schemes on which I have expended so much time and trouble," he said, "and yet I cannot refute your arguments. Who taught you such things?"

"Perhaps suffering as I have these past years," Lalitha answered. "I have learnt that what everyone really wants in life is happiness. People think it comes from success, money, or Social position!"

She paused to go on:

"That may be true for a few, but I believe they are exceptional. Ordinary people are really seeking love and they can find it only when they are safe and secure, not harassed and hunted or terror-stricken, for there can be no happiness in . . . fear."

There was a note of passionate intensity in Lalitha's voice and Lord Rothwyn said:

"Let me ask you a question, Lalitha. Have you been happier, if not happy, these past weeks?"

"They have been more wonderful than I could ever explain to you," Lalitha answered. "It is as if you brought me out of a deep, dark dungeon where there was no light, no hope, into the sun-shine."

"Thank you," Lord Rothwyn said softly.

As if she felt shy at speaking so intimately, Lalitha looked at the plans on the desk and asked:

"Will you take me this afternoon, as you promised, to see your Elizabethan house?"

"I meant to do that," Lord Rothwyn said, "but I am going to ask you if you will excuse me, Lalitha, and let me take you tomorrow. I had forgotten an appointment in London which I think I ought to keep."

He saw the disappointment on her face and said:

"I gave my promise and so I think you will be the first to agree that I should keep it."

The curiosity in her eyes made him continue:

"A friend of mine, Henry Grey Bennet, is Chairman of a Parliamentary Select Committee. It deals with a number of injustices and various disorders, including the terrible traffic which is taking place at the moment in shipping young girls, many of them little more than children, to the Continent."

Lalitha's eyes widened as she asked:

"What for?"

Lord Rothwyn chose his words with care:

"They are sold into what amounts to slavery," he answered. "There are places in Amsterdam where English girls can be bought by the highest bidder as if they were cattle. Some of them are taken even further afield, to countries like Morocco, Turkey, and Egypt."

"And the girls have no choice in the matter?"

"None at all!" Lord Rothwyn replied. "Many of them are kidnapped from off the streets. There is, I understand from my friend, a number of women who meet young girls when they come up from the country, at Coaching-Inns."

"Why do they listen to strangers?"

"They have never been to London before and when a kind person offers them a bed for the night or the chance of lucrative employment, they agree eagerly—never to be heard of again!"

"How horrifying!" Lalitha exclaimed.

"This traffic is assuming such proportions," Lord Rothwyn said, "that it is time that something is done about it officially. At the moment the law is very lax and those who operate what is called the 'White Slave Trade' are seldom brought to justice."

"And do you think you can get a new law passed to prevent it?" Lalitha asked.

"My friend's Bill has been accepted by the House of Commons," Lord Rothwyn said. "This afternoon it comes before the House of Lords."

He paused to add:

"My friend is not very confident of success, so I think, as I promised I would support it, I should go to London."

"But of course you must!" Lalitha agreed. "It is important, very important! I cannot bear to think of those poor girls."

She paused for a moment and then asked in a low voice:

"Are they badly . . . treated?"

"If they do not do what is required of them," Lord Rothwyn said, "they are beaten or drugged into submission."

He saw the little shudder that went through Lalitha before she said:

"Then you must try to get the Act passed."

"I will do my best," Lord Rothwyn said, "but it means that I should leave for London almost immediately."

"You will be back tonight?"

"I hope quite early in the evening," he answered, "but definitely in time for dinner. Shall we dine together?"

"Could I do that?" Lalitha asked. "And I could wear one of my new gowns?"

"We will make a party of it," Lord Rothwyn told her with a smile. "Your first evening downstairs. I think that calls for a celebration!"

Lalitha put up her hands, laughing.

"You are only making it an excuse to stuff me with more food," she said. "I am getting so fat that all my beautiful new gowns will have to be let out!"

"When that happens I will buy you more!" Lord Rothwyn promised.

Lalitha hesitated a moment and then she said in a low voice:

"I would not . . . wish Your Lordship to . . . spend too much . . . money on me."

He smiled as he replied:

"I promise you that what I have spent will not bankrupt me!"

"You have given me . . . so much," Lalitha said, "I do not know how to . . . thank you."

"Shall we talk about it at dinner?" he asked. "I will leave Royal and the other dogs to look after you."

Lalitha bent down to pat Royal, who had unobtrusively laid himself down at her feet.

"I am sure they will take care of me," she said, "until . . . you return."

All the same, she found that when Lord Rothwyn had gone she missed him.

Somehow the house seemed empty.

She had a strange, unaccountable feeling of loneliness that had not been there before.

She went with the dogs into the garden and admired the smooth lawns which were like velvet, the long flower-beds, filled with colour, which somehow reminded her of the great Picture Gallery inside the house.

She lingered outside the yew-hedged maze, afraid to go in alone in case she should lose her way.

She wandered down to the gold-fish pond which lay in a secret garden enclosed behind red brick Elizabethan walls.

It was all very lovely, the sun-shine was warm on her head, but she knew that she was counting the hours until Lord Rothwyn returned home.

'It is because I am so anxious to hear if he has been successful in helping to pass the Act he is supporting,' she thought.

But she knew the truth was that she wanted to know he was beside her and to talk with him on all the topics that appeared to interest them both.

Not wishing to tire herself before the evening, she went in from the garden and sat down to try and piece together the pieces of paper on which Lord Hadley had written his poem over three hundred years ago.

It was amazing that so much remained of his efforts despite the ravages of vermin.

Fortunately he had written on very thick and expensive parchment and his writing was firm and neatly formed. But the S's were made as F's, and piecing together even two or three pieces took a long time.

Lalitha had managed what appeared to be almost one sentence and was elated with her progress when the door opened and a footman said:

"Miss Studley to see you, M'Lady!"

Lalitha gave a little cry which rose irrepressibly to her lips and as she sprang to her feet she saw standing in the doorway Sophie.

She was looking entrancingly lovely in a travelling-gown of sky blue silk and a small bonnet trimmed with rose-buds.

She was smiling, but Lalitha trembled as she walked across the room.

"Are you surprised to see me?" Sophie asked.

"Y-yes!" Lalitha managed to answer.

"I wanted to have a talk with you," Sophie said, "and I knew you would be alone this afternoon so I came here by carriage."

"H-how did you . . . know that?"

Lalitha suddenly felt stupid and her teeth seemed almost to be chattering.

"It was reported in the morning newspapers that Lord Rothwyn was to speak this afternoon in the House of Lords," Sophie replied. "That gave us an opportunity to have a little chat."

Lalitha did not answer and Sophie looked round her.

"What a very pleasant room!" she said. "May I sit down?"

"Yes . . . yes, of course!" Lalitha faltered. "I am sorry . . . but I am surprised at seeing you."

"I thought you would be interested to hear how I was," Sophie said. "But do not be afraid, Lalitha, Mama is not angry with you."

"N-not . . . a-angry?" Lalitha stammered.

"No. She understands that you could not help what you did," Sophie said, "if in fact you are married to Lord Rothwyn, as he told me in the letter that I received."

"He wrote to . . . you?"

"Yes," Sophie answered. "Yet strangely enough there has been no announcement of your marriage and no-one has been notified of it except me!"

Lalitha made no reply and Sophie went on:

"It leads me to think it is only a temporary arrangement you are enjoying here. Is that so?"

"I do not . . . know," Lalitha answered.

"Let me tell you the truth, Lalitha," Sophie went on.

"I love Lord Rothwyn, I always have! When I knew I had lost him, I realised that I had lost everything that mattered to me in life!"

Lalitha stared at Sophie in astonishment.

"But you never . . . appeared to . . . love him," she protested. "You said you were . . . marrying him only because he was . . . wealthy."

"I suppose I was shy at confessing to you how deeply my feelings were involved," Sophie said, "and as I have already said, it was only after you had left to tell him that I must keep my promise to Julius that I faced the truth!"

Lalitha sat bewildered.

She could hardly credit that Sophie had really changed her mind, and yet she had never before heard her speak with such emotion.

"What about . . . Mr. Verton?" she enquired.

"Julius never received the note that I wrote to him," Sophie replied, "and so he is at my feet, wanting us to marry more ardently than ever before."

"Then why are you not married?" Lalitha asked. "The wedding should have taken place nearly two weeks ago."

"It was not the Duke who died," Sophie answered. "That was just a joke on the part of Lord Rothwyn and not one in particularly good taste. But an Aunt of whom Julius was very fond did pass away and therefore out of decency our wedding must be postponed for two months."

"Oh, I see!" Lalitha exclaimed. "And in the . . . meantime you have . . . realised that you love . . . Lord Rothwyn."

"That is right!" Sophie agreed, "and so I am asking you Lalitha, to give me back what has always belonged to me."

"I do not . . . understand."

"It is quite simple," Sophie answered. "Lord Rothwyn loves me, as you well know."

"He was . . . angry with . . . you," Lalitha said. "That is why he . . . made me take . . . your place . . . forced me to do so."

"In revenge," Sophie said with a light laugh, "and he

made that very clear in his letter! But you cannot imagine for one moment, Lalitha, that he wished to marry anyone but me! He adores me! He worships me! And really love does not change over-night!"

"No . . . I . . . suppose . . . not," Lalitha said almost beneath her breath.

"I therefore have a very sensible plan," Sophie said, "and one which has Mama's full approval."

"What is . . . that?" Lalitha asked apprehensively.

"It is that you should leave here at once," Sophie answered. "Mama was sure that you would wish to join your old Nurse, of whom you were always so fond. She has therefore sent you a present of twenty pounds—think of it, Lalitha—twenty pounds! It is a lot of money!"

"I cannot just . . . leave like . . . that," Lalitha protested. "His Lordship has been so . . . kind and he has made me . . . well."

"I know exactly what he has done," Sophie said, and for the first time her voice was hard.

"You . . . you know?" Lalitha enquired.

"There are people who are prepared to tell us exactly what goes on!"

"Do you mean the . . . servants?"

"There is no need for us to go into details," Sophie replied evasively. "What I am suggesting, Lalitha, is common sense, as I am sure you will see. You cannot inflict yourself on Lord Rothwyn forever, now can you?"

"N-no."

"So instead of embarrassing him by hanging about when he has no reason for keeping you now that I am back in his life," Sophie said, "and ready to give him everything he asks of me, it would be best for you to disappear."

"I would wish to say . . . good-bye, and thank him."

"What for?" Sophie asked. "He has used you deliberately to hurt me. You were a tool—a weapon he had at hand at that particular moment. If I had sent a maid-servant in your place, exactly the same thing would have happened."

There was a pause and Sophie went on:

"But you would not wish to embarrass Lord Rothwyn by making him dismiss you as if you were in fact a servant!"

Her eyes were on Lalitha's face as she continued:

"I thought you would desire to behave like a lady. That is why Mama has sent you this money, so that you can show some dignity in what has been a most unfortunate circumstance."

Lalitha made a helpless little gesture and asked:

"What do you . . . want me to . . . do?"

"I want you to put a few things together," Sophie replied, "only what you can carry under your cloak without being observed, and ostensibly we will set off for a short drive. My carriage is outside."

"And . . . then?"

"I will take you to the nearest cross-roads where the stage-coaches stop on their way to London. When you reach Charing Cross you can take another coach which will carry you to Norwich."

Her voice was firm as she continued:

"There are always two in the day and if you hurry you will catch the evening one. Once there, I imagine you can find your way to your Nurse. Mama was certain you know where is is staying."

"Yes . . . of course . . . I do."

"Then what are you worrying about?"

"It is just that I do not . . . know if I am doing the . . . right thing," Lalitha said unhappily.

"When Lord Rothwyn realises I have come to him to give him my heart, and that I am ready to be his wife," Sophie said softly, "he will no longer wish to be troubled with you."

Lalitha gave a deep sigh which seemed to come from the very depths of her being.

"No . . . I suppose you are . . . right."

"I will come upstairs with you while you put on your cloak," Sophie said. "Do not leave any messages with servants. Do not write anything. There is no point in making things more difficult for him than they are already. It is natural he would feel under an obligation to stop you."

"But we were . . . married!" Lalitha said in a low voice.

Sophie gave a little laugh.

"A marriage which for a few pounds can be obliterated from the Vicar's memory and the evidence removed from the Marriage Register."

Lalitha's eyes went to Sophie's and she cried involuntarily:

"You have . . . already done that!"

"Yes, I have already done it!" Sophie answered. "It was quite easy. There was no-one in the Church when I walked into the Vestry. The Register was open on a table. I tore out the page. No-one will ever know that you went through a form of marriage with a man who was heart-broken because you were not the bride he had anticipated!"

Lalitha shut her eyes. For a moment it seemed as if there was nothing she could say.

Once again Sophie was doing exactly as she wanted and there was no gain-saying her.

They walked up the stairs to Lalitha's bed-room. There was no-one there at this time of the afternoon.

Nattie would be in her own room and there were no house-maids in attendance unless the bell was rung for them.

Sophie opened the wardrobe doors.

"His Lordship has certainy fitted you out well!" she said sharply. "It is fortunate we can both wear the same clothes."

"I am afraid those gowns will be much too tight for you," Lalitha said. "I am very much thinner than you are."

"Then they can be thrown away," Sophie retorted airily. "You cannot take them with you. It would seem far too suspicious if the footmen had to carry a trunk downstairs."

"Yes . . . of course," Lalitha agreed.

She took a night-gown and some under-clothes from the drawers and put them into a soft, silk shawl which she laid open on the bed.

She added a hair-brush. Then she hesitated, thinking

that she would wish to take at least one dress with her, but Sophie said:

"That is enough, Lalitha. Even what you have collected may look bulky under your cloak."

Obediently, because there seemed to be nothing else she could do, Lalitha rolled up the things in the shawl and then took down from the wardrobe a thin travelling-cloak that she had worn the first time she had gone into the garden.

Sophie opened the cupboard in which Lalitha's bonnets and hats were kept and which matched the various gowns which had been sent down from London.

"These are entrancing!" she exclaimed.

"Perhaps I had better wear one," Lalitha suggested.

"Why? Sophie asked. "You can pull the hood of your cloak up over your hair. The servants will not think it strange, as you are only going for a drive with me and you would not wish to look conspicious on the stage-coach."

Lalitha knew that Sophie was saying this only because she wished to keep the bonnets and hats for herself. But there seemed to be no point in arguing.

She had to leave, and when she was with her old Nurse in Norfolk she would certainly have no occasion to wear the elegant, expensive creations which had come from Bond Street.

"Here is your money!" Sophie said abruptly.

She held out a small purse.

Lalitha took it from her reluctantly.

She would have liked to say that she would take nothing from Sophie or her mother. Then she told herself practically that she could not inflict herself on her old Nurse, who had little to spare as it was.

She put the little purse into an elegant ridicule of heavy satin, added a handkerchief, and picked up a pair of suede gloves.

Sophie looked at her.

"You certainly look better than you used to," she said. "I should imagine you will be able to get work of some sort, wherever you live."

"Yes . . . of course," Lalitha said automatically and

added: "That reminds me. I will take some needles and embroidery silks with me."

She drew them out of a drawer, thinking with a little throb of her heart as she did so that she had persuaded Nattie to give them to her so that she could start to embroider a monogram on His Lordship's handker-chiefs.

They were all together in a little bag with her thimble and a pair of scissors.

"Come on!" Sophie said impatiently. "If you remember all the things you need we shall take half the house with us!"

Lalitha looked round the room in which she had slowly come back to health. It seemed a haven of security and peace.

Now she must leave it forever for an unknown future.

She suddenly felt desperately afraid.

She was going back into a world which she had thought would no longer menace her. She was leaving Lord Rothwyn, who had said he would protect her!

"Do hurry!" Sophie cried impatiently. "You will miss the stage-coach and then you will have to stay the night in London."

Lalitha felt a little tremor of fear.

Supposing she encountered one of the women who Lord Rothwyn had told her waited to kidnap unsuspecting girls from the country and spirited them away into slavery over-seas?

She felt in a panic that she could not go! She must stay here!

She thought that she would run to Nattie and tell her what Sophie was making her do and plead for her help.

Then she knew she could not lower herself to behave in such a manner.

Sophie was right. Lord Rothwyn had been kind but he was not really interested in her. It was Sophie he wanted.

If Sophie was now ready to love him as he wished to be loved, he would be happy.

Without speaking she followed Sophie downstairs and into the Hall.

The Major-Domo came forward as they turned towards the front door and said to Lalitha:

"You are going driving, M'Lady?"

"We are going for a short drive," Sophie answered before Lalitha could speak. "We shall be back very shortly."

"Very good, Miss," the Major-Domo answered, and added to Lalitha:

"Will you be taking Royal with you, M'Lady?"

For the first time Lalitha realised that Royal was at her heels. She picked him up in her arms.

Here was something else it was hard to leave. She loved the little dog.

For a moment she held him close against her heart and kissed his soft, silky head.

Then she handed him to the Major-Domo.

"Take him to Nattie," she said.

She heard Royal whine as she turned away to walk down the steps.

The footman opened the door of the carriage, a rug was placed solicitiously over their knees, and the horses started off.

"I am going away," Lalitha told herself, and it was like the point of a dagger being driven into her breast.

"I shall never come back! I shall never see him again."

The horses, gathering speed, moved from the courtyard and onto the drive.

Lalitha looked back.

The house in the afternoon sun-shine looked very beautiful. It was magnificent and at the same time she knew that it had been a haven of security which had encircled her like protective arms.

Now she was leaving.

"Good-bye . . . my love," she whispered beneath her breath.

As the words came to her lips she knew that it was not the house to which she was saying good-bye, but to its owner.

Chapter Five

Lord Rothwyn walked from the Chamber of the House of Lords. His friend Henry Grey Bennet was waiting for him.

"I am sorry, Henry," he said.

"It was only what I expected," Mr. Bennet answered, "but I shall try again, make no mistake! I shall try and go on trying to get this Bill passed."

"And I will support you," Lord Rothwyn promised.

"You did your best. That was an excellent and most eloquent speech of yours. "

"Thank you."

"Where shall we drown our sorrows? Here or at White's?" Henry Grey Bennet asked.

Lord Rothwyn hesitated for a moment.

Then as he was about to accept the suggestion he had an inescapable feeling that he should go back to Roth Park.

He could not explain it to himself. He just knew that there was a sudden urgency in him to go home.

"Forgive me, Henry, another time," he replied. "I came up from the country especially to speak, as I promised you I would, and now I must get back."

"It is unlike you to be in the country at this time of the year," his friend remarked. "You missed the racing at Ascot."

There was no answer because Lord Rothwyn had already left him and was proceeding to where outside the House of Lords his curricle was waiting.

Drawn by four horses of superlative blood-stock, he could travel the miles to Roth Park quicker than anyone else had ever managed to do.

In fact Lord Rothwyn had already set several records.

As he climbed into the curricle he remembered with a faint twinge of conscience that he had intended to call at Carlton House.

The Regent had returned to London from Brighton to attend the Christening at Kensington Palace of the daughter of the Duke and Duchess of Kent.

She had been baptised Alexandrina Victoria.

Lord Rothwyn was well aware that His Royal Highness would think it extremely off-hand of him not to have made at least an appearance while he was in London.

He knew that His Highness was longing to discuss with him the alterations and additions to the Royal Pavilion at Brighton.

Owing to national and political criticism, work had ceased until the Queen, impressed by her son's vision of an Indian Palace, had contributed fifty thousand pounds from her own pocket.

Even so, the ornate domes, the Indian columns, graceful colonnades, piece-stone lattice work, delicate cornices, and fretted battlements had cost a fortune.

The huge chandeliers like water-lilies, the Chinese landscapes of scarlet, gold, and yellow lacquer in the Music-Room, and the spreading palm tree with a silver dragon among the leaves in the Banqueting-Room swelled the total.

Lord Rothwyn knew thirty-three thousand pounds had been spent last year and that it was likely to be forty thousand pounds this.

He did however like the Regent as a man and admired what he was trying to create with a sense of fantasy and a romantic exuberance unknown in a Royal Monarch since Charles I.

"People abuse me and mock the Pavilion," His Royal Highness had said bitterly to Lord Rothwyn on his last visit to Brighton.

"Posterity will admire your improvement to London, Sire," Lord Rothwyn answered, "and one day the Royal Pavilion will be the greatest sight in Brighton."

Yet despite all the arguments in his mind that to call on the Regent would be the right thing to do, Lord Rothwyn wanted to reach Roth Park.

He therefore settled himself down to driving his horses with an expertise which made him one of the outstanding Corinthians of the era.

His groom sitting up behind the curricule noted with satisfaction that as they passed everyone's head was turned admiringly in their direction.

It would have been impossible not to admire Lord Rothwyn.

He was not only handsome, but with his high hat at an angle he had a presence which complemented the smartness and magnificence of his horses.

The houses were soon left behind and they were in the open country.

Lord Rothwyn gave his team their head and they travelled what to other people might have seemed an incredible pace along the road North which went through Barnet and Potters Bar, eventually emerging into a valley above which Roth Park was situated.

The great house was looking superb in the warmth of the evening sun-shine, which made the red bricks glow as if they were precious jewels.

The flag was flying above the high roof-line, which was one of the finest characteristics of the building, and below it the lake gleamed gold as the white swans moved with grace across its surface.

As always when he saw the house, Lord Rothwyn felt a pride not only of ownership, but because he was descended from a long line of intelligent, creative ancestors.

He drove up to the front door with a flourish, pulled his horses to a stand-still, and turned to smile at the groom behind him.

"Better than usual, Ned?" he asked. It was a question.

"Three minutes quicker than our last journey, M'Lord."

"That is good, Ned."

"It is indeed, M'Lord."

Lord Rothwyn walked up the flight of stone steps to where the Major-Domo was waiting for him.

As he took His Lordship's hat and driving-gloves the Major-Domo said:

"There's a lady to see you in the Silver Salon, M'Lord."

"A lady?" Lord Rothwyn queried.

"A Miss Studley, M'Lord."

For a moment Lord Rothwyn was still. Then there was a scowl between his eyes as he walked across the Hall.

A footman opened the door to the Silver Salon and he entered to find Sophie standing at the window.

She had removed her bonnet and the sunshine was dazzling on her gold hair.

It also revealed the perfection of her pink and white skin, the liquid blue of her eyes, and the classical curves of her rosebud mouth.

She turned at his entrance and with a little cry of pleasure ran towards him.

"Inigo!" she exclaimed.

"What are you doing here?"

The question was sharp and abrupt.

Sophie came to a stop in front of him and raised her eyes to his.

"Need you ask that question?" she enquired.

Then as Lord Rothwyn stared at her without speaking she put out her white arms towards him as if she would place them round his neck.

"I had to come, Inigo!" she said dramatically. "I had to!"

"May I ask what you mean by that?" he enquired.

She would have pressed herself close to him, but he walked away from her to stand on the hearth with his back to the mantel-piece.

"I did not invite you."

"I know that," she replied softly, "but I could go on no longer without seeing you. So I drove here this afternoon."

"We have nothing to say to each other," Lord Rothwyn declared. "Nothing at all!"

"I have a lot to say," Sophie said in a beguiling tone.

She had drawn near to him as she spoke and now once again she was standing beside him.

"I love you!" she said. "I have only just realised how much I love you, and how I cannot live without you."

Lord Rothwyn looked down at her and his lips twisted in a cynical smile as he asked:

"Now what can have provoked such an outburst of

passion? Can it be the fact that Verton has left for the Continent?"

He saw a little flicker in Sophie's eyes which told him that she had not expected him to know this, but the tone of her voice did not change as she said:

"I made a mistake, Inigo, when I sent Lalitha to you that night, or rather Mama made me. You know how she forbade me even to think of marriage where you were concerned."

"So it was your mother who forced you to jilt me at the last moment?" Lord Rothwyn said slowly.

"Yes, yes, it was Mama! You know how dictatorial she is, and I could not disobey her. I love you—and I told her so—but she would not listen."

Lord Rothwyn's eyes were hard as he said:

"You are a good actress, Sophie, but not good enough. I am well aware why you have come here today. Verton has talked and Society is not smiling so kindly upon you as it once did."

"That is not true!" Sophie said quickly. "And anyway it is of no consequence. I love you and that is all that matters!"

"Even though I am not a Duke?" Lord Rothwyn asked cynically.

"I never wanted to marry Julius. Mama made me and while he was in England I did not dare to get in touch with you. Now that he has left, I am free. Free to come to you as I wish to do."

"Cannot even you see that it is too late for you to 'change your mind' as you call it?" Lord Rothwyn asked. "As you well know, I am married."

He paused a moment and then he said:

"Have you seen Lalitha? What have you said to her?"

"Lalitha has been very accommodating," Sophie replied. "She will not interfere with our plans in any way."

"What plans?" Lord Rothwyn enquired. "I will not have Lalitha upset!"

His hand went towards the bell-pull as if he would ring it, and as she realised his intention Sophie said quickly:

"Do not ring for Lalitha. She has left!"

"Left? What do you mean left?"

Lord Rothwyn's question was sharp.

"I told her how much I loved you," Sophie explained, "and she agreed to go out of your life. After all, you only married her out of revenge—to punish me."

"Lalitha agreed to go out of my life?" Lord Rothwyn said slowly, as if he could hardly understand the words. "But how? And where has she gone?"

"She will not trouble you anymore," Sophie answered. "I have made arrangements for her future. She will be quite all right. You need not think of her again."

"Where has she gone?" Lord Rothwyn asked.

"Surely it is immaterial?" Sophie said. "You have not announced your marriage to her, so no-one in London is aware that it ever happened. I am prepared to marry you as soon as it can be arranged, tomorrow or the next day. Then we can be together as you always wanted."

Her voice died away as she realised that Lord Rothwyn's face had suddenly become contorted wtih an anger that was frightening.

"Do you imagine," he said firmly, "that I would touch you, let alone marry you, after the manner in which you and your mother treated Lalitha?"

"It was nothing to do with me," Sophie said quickly, "and if she has told you a lot of lies, you need not believe them. She always was a liar and a cheat. After all, she is nothing but a love-child. My mother looked after her out of charity."

"Where has she gone?"

"Why are you so interested in her?" Sophie enquired. "She is a nobody—ugly and emaciated! I am prepared to give you myself, Inigo. Could you ask for anything more?"

"You revolt me!" Lord Rothwyn retorted, "and although I have no desire to touch you, if you do not tell me where Lalitha has gone I will throttle the truth out of you, or I will beat you in the same manner that your mother beat that wretched girl!"

He spoke with such ferocity that Sophie instinctively moved backwards.

"You must be mad to speak to me like that!"

"I will speak to you in a far worse manner if you do not answer my question! Where is Lalitha? Must I repeat myself, or shall I force an answer from you?"

He took a step towards her and now Sophie was really frightened.

She gave a little cry.

"Do not touch me! I will tell you! I will tell you where Lalitha has gone."

"Very well," Lord Rothwyn said, "and hurry up about it!"

"I gave Lalitha money to go Norfolk," she said. "I do not know exactly where but she left on the stage-coach."

"At the cross-roads?"

"I took her there."

"That is all I wanted to know," Lord Rothwyn said.

He walked towards the door.

As he reached it he turned back to say:

"Get out of my house! If I find you here when I return I will order the servants to throw you out!"

He left the Salon, slamming the door behind him.

As he reached the Hall the Major-Domo looked at his furious face apprehensively but he walked past him and round to the Stables.

"My curricule with four fresh horses immediately!" Lord Rothwyn ordered.

"Very good, M'Lord."

Half a dozen grooms ran to do his bidding and although Lord Rothwyn waited with obvious impatience it was less than four minutes before the curricle was ready, drawn by a team of well-matched chestnuts.

Lord Rothwyn flung himself into the driving-seat and the horses were already moving before Ned had scrambled up behind.

If he had driven quickly from London it was nothing compared to the speed he achieved now.

Only when they reached the cross-roads did he slacken his pace to ask:

"Which way would the afternoon stage-coach travel to London?"

"That'll be the slow one, M'Lord, stopping at the smaller villages. Your Lordship goes left."

Lord Rothwyn took the left fork and once again, despite the fact that the road twisted and turned, he managed to proceed at a speed which occasionally made Ned grip the sides and press his lips together in consternation.

Never had he known His Lordship to push his horses so hard.

Even so the evening was drawing on and they were within a few miles of London when ahead they saw a heavy, ponderous stage-coach packed with passengers.

It carried on top an assorted collection of baggage, including several hen-coops and a young goat sewn into a sack.

As the road was narrow it took Lord Rothwyn some time before he was able to pass the coach.

Only then was he able to bring his sweating team to a stand-still across the road so that the stage-coach was obliged to come to a halt.

"Wot d'ye think ye're a-doing of?" the coach-man shouted truculently.

"Her Ladyship will be inside, Ned," Lord Rothwyn said. "Ask her to join me."

"Very good, M'Lord."

Ned climbed down from the curricle and ran to the coach.

The coach-man and the man up on the box shouted abuse at him, but he paid no attention and pulled open the heavy door.

Packed in amongst fat farmers, small children, a Parson, and two commercial travelers, he saw Lalitha.

She was sitting with her head bent, her hood pulled low over her forehead so that those in the coach could not see her tears.

It had been impossible not to cry as the coach took her further and further away from everything that meant security and happiness.

As they had driven through the great stone gates of Roth Park and reached the open road Lalitha admitted to herself that she was leaving behind the man she loved.

She had loved him, she thought, since the moment he kissed her in the Church-yard thinking she was Sophie.

She had loved him although she had been frightened of him when he had come to her room and she had thought he was the most handsome man she had ever seen in her life.

It was not only his looks; there was something else about him to which she instinctively reached out.

She could not explain it.

It was as if something secret within her recognised in him all that she longed for in life.

Even alone in her beautiful bed-room she had been conscious that the house, the furnishings, the pictures, all were a part of him.

Just as his ancestor had built into the house his mind, his imagination, and heart, so Lord Rothwyn had imprinted his personality on it.

Then when they had talked together and Lord Rothwyn had shown her his possessions he had been kind and gentle in a manner which she had never expected from any man, let alone from him.

She recognised now that she had lost her heart hopelessly and irretrievably.

"I love him! I love him!" she whispered, "and now I shall never see him again!"

It demanded a tremendous effort of self-control not to cry until Sophie had dropped her at the cross-roads.

"Good-bye, Lalitha," she had said as the stage-coach lumbered into sight. "Do not forget your promise to forget that mock-marriage to Lord Rothwyn and all that has happened since. He will not remember your existence and neither shall I!"

Lalitha did not answer but merely stepped out of Sophie's carriage carrying her small bundle under her arm and with some difficulty a place was found for her in the already over-crowded coach.

Sophie did not wait to see her go.

As soon as Lalitha was on the road the coach-man turned back the way they had come—back towards Roth Park.

It was hot and noisy inside the coach. There was a smell of food and smoke and sweat, but Lalitha could think only of Sophie's beauty as Lord Rothwyn would see her when he returned that evening.

She thought of him walking into the house, the dogs running to greet him. Then he would find waiting for him not herself, as he would have expected, but Sophie.

She could imagine his arms going round her, Sophie's lovely face turned up to his, and then he would kiss her.

The thought, the pain of it, was an agony within her breast that she had not believed possible.

It was worse than the pain she had endured from her Step-mother's beatings; worse than anything she had ever suffered before.

Lalitha shut her eyes.

"How can I bear to think of it for the rest of my life?" she asked and then the tears came.

She wiped them away surreptitiously but she could not check them.

The stage-coach rumbled on, stopping at one small village and then another.

Some passengers got out, others got in, and goods were taken down from the roof.

It caused an inordinate amount of noise, shouting, heavy thumpings, and occasionally a bleat from the goat.

On again.

Still Lalitha could think of nothing but Lord Rothwyn; the way he had talked to her with sympathy and understanding, and the occasional look in his eyes which would make her draw in her breath and find it difficult to speak.

Had he any fondness for her at all? she wondered. Or had she just been an encumbrance—someone forced upon him by chance and whom he would be glad to see go?

Again it was an agony to think that she had meant nothing!

Then sharply she tried to rally her pride and the courage she had always thought she possessed.

She must face facts. She was of no consequence to him, a woman he would never even have encountered had it not been for Sophie's perfidy.

He had been sorry for her, that was obvious, but how was it conceivable that he could have any other feeling for someone so unattractive?

Lalitha told herself than anyone who had looked at Sophie's incredibly breath-taking beauty would be immune to the attraction of other women however fascinating.

As she herself had no attractions at all she could certainly not be facinating to someone as fastidious as Lord Rothwyn.

She had always guessed that there had been many other women in his life, and if she had not, Nattie's chatter would not have left her long in ignorance.

"He's had too much in life, His Lordship has!" she said once. "Spoilt he's been ever since he was a small boy by every one who admired him."

"Was he always so handsome?" Lalitha asked.

"The most beautiful child I've ever seen, like a little angel!" Nettie answered. "And when he grew older he stood out in any company. No wonder the ladies were always after him!"

"Were . . . they?" Lalitha asked in a low voice.

"But of course," Nettie replied. "With His Lordship's looks, his position and his wealth, he is every young girl's dream and the match every mother wants for her daughter."

"It is strange that he has not married before," Lalitha said.

"That's what I've often said to him," Nattie said, "but he always laughs and says: 'I have not yet found a woman to come up to my ideal!' "

Eventually he found her, Lalitha thought with a little sob. He found Sophie, who was as beautiful in her way as His Lordship was handsome in his.

"An ideal couple!" She could imagine the excitement their marriage would cause in the *Beau Monde*.

He would take Sophie to Carlton House. She would grace the Opening of Parliament and be without exception the most beautiful Peeress at the Coronation.

Lalitha fought back her sobs.

"Why, oh why," she asked in her heart, "could I not have fallen in love with an ordinary man? Someone of no Social consequence who might perhaps have loved me and we could have found happiness together in a cottage?"

But, no, she had had to love a man who was as far beyond her as the stars in the sky!

"How can you be so foolish?" How can you be so foolish?" the wheels of the coach seemed to say to Lalitha as they rumbled over the dusty roads.

Her answer seemed also to repeat itself over and over again.

"I cannot help it! I cannot help it!"

The tears were wet on her cheeks when unaccountably the coach came to a sudden stand-still.

She could hear the coach-man shouting outside and one of the passengers, an elderly farmer, said angrily:

"What be we stopping for now? Us be late enough already."

"It's disgraceful that these coaches never run to time," a tight-lipped, middle-aged man who was obviously a clerk said sharply.

As he spoke the door was opened and a groom with a high cockaded hat and crested silver buttons on his livery put his head inside.

He looked round at the passengers, saw Lalitha, and said:

" 'is Lordship be waiting outside, M'Lady."

Her head came up quickly.

For a moment she stared at him incredulously, and then she said hesitatingly:

"H-His . . . Lordship?"

" 'e be waiting, M'Lady."

The other passengers had been stunned into silence at this exchange.

Now the clerk who had been complaining said:

"If you be getting out, Ma'am, we'd be obliged if you'd do it sharpish like. All these delays are a-making us extremely late."

"I am sorry," Lalitha tried to say.

She had some difficulty in disentangling herself from

the two passengers on either side of her and even more in stepping across the legs of those between her and the door.

Ned helped her down into the road and she saw ahead the four horses drawn across the highway to prevent the coach from proceeding.

On the curricule the driver wore his hat at an angle she could not fail to recognise.

Her heart was beating suffocatingly as she walked towards him. When she reached the curricule Ned helped her into it.

She sat down beside Lord Rothwyn and the groom covered her gown with a light rug.

Then the horses were moving and Ned had sprung up behind them.

For a moment it was impossible for Lalitha to look at Lord Rothwyn and she was acutely conscious that anything they said could be over-heard.

After a moment when he did not speak to her she stole a glance at him.

His face was in profile, and yet it was impossible not to see the scowl between his eyes and that his mouth was set in a hard line.

Now she felt as if an icy hand squeezed the blood from her heart. He was angry! Angry with her and yet she had done what she thought was right for him; what would bring him happiness!

Lord Rothwyn drove on until they reached a village green where he was able to turn his horses. Then they were forced to wait for the stage-coach to pass them.

The sun which had been sinking in a blaze of glory disappeared over the horizon and it was growing dusk.

The road back towards Roth Park looked shadowy and indistinct.

"Why did you leave?" Lord Rothwyn asked before re-starting his team.

"I . . . I . . . thought you w-would . . . no longer . . . want me to s-stay," Lalitha stammered.

It was difficult for her to speak clearly because she was so disturbed by his anger and by the hard note in his voice.

"Did you want to go?" he enquired.

Then as she looked at him in bewilderment that he should ask such a question, he saw the tear-stains on her cheeks and that her long eye-lashes were wet.

Quite suddenly he smiled and the darkness was gone from his face as he said:

"Have you not learnt by this time that I never leave unfinished a building on which I am working?"

There was no longer a pain within her breast and she was no longer frightened.

A wave of incredible happiness swept over her, but before she could answer him he had tightened the reins and the horses mover forward.

"He is taking me back!" Lalitha told herself. "Back . . . home!"

She hardly dared think the word—let alone say it, even to herself.

The horses were travelling quickly, but not as quickly as they had on the outward journey. Yet it still seemed to Lalitha to be very fast after the lumbering of the over-laden stage-coach.

There was no longer the smell, the heat, and the close proximity of the passengers.

There was a wind in her face and something like a wild elation in her heart.

There was no need for words.

She could only feel that once again Lord Rothwyn had taken her out of a deep, dark dungeon into the light and she was blinded by it.

They were held up while a herd of cows who had obviously been to a farm to be milked crossed the road back to the fields.

"You are all right?" Lord Rothwyn asked.

"Yes . . . quite all . . . right."

Her misery had vanished, everything seemed light and wonderful. She was beside him and that was all she asked of life.

It was growing darker and the sky was not as clear as it had been all day. Clouds were gathering, a prelude to rain.

What was more, they were in forest land on a narrow

road winding and twisting between high, dark trees on either side of it, so that it was dangerous to proceed quickly.

They were in fact moving quite slowly when as they rounded a corner there came a shout from the right-hand side of the road.

As Lord Rothwyn instinctively pulled in his horses two men on horse-back appeared in front of them.

"Stand and deliver!"

Lalitha gave a gasp.

She saw Lord Rothwyn turn his head to look at the masked highwayman on his side of the curricule.

Then he put down his hand. In a pocket there was a pistol which was always kept loaded for emergencies such as this.

Even as he grasped it the highwayman fired and he fell backwards with a bullet through his shoulder.

Lalitha gave a terrified scream as Lord Rothwyn dropped the reins and put his left hand up to his wounded arm.

"Ye'll keep still if ye knows wat's good for ye!" the highwayman snarled in a coarse voice.

"Get 'em off th' road!" another voice ordered, and Lalitha turned to find that there was yet another highwayman on their left.

"Four men against two," she thought despairingly, and Lord Rothwyn already wounded.

The highwayman who had fired came nearer and now with his horse alongside the carriage leant over to look at his victim.

Lord Rothwyn's hat had fallen off with the impact of the shot, but he was sitting upright again and his eyes met those of the highwayman defiantly.

"Damn you!" he said. "What the devil do you want? We have little of value with us."

The highwayman smiled unpleasantly.

"We be urgently in need o' new horse-flesh."

"Curse you!" Lord Rothwyn expostulated furiously.

As he spoke Lalitha saw the highwayman turn the pistol he held in his hand round until he was holding it by the barrel.

He raised it and she knew that he was about to

strike Lord Rothwyn on the head and there was nothing he could do about it. He was at a lower level than the highwayman on his horse and already wounded.

She rose to her feet and put her hands protectively over Lord Rothwyn's head.

"No!" she cried desperately. "No! You cannot do that!"

"Why not?" the highwayman asked.

For a moment she thought that she could not speak, then in a voice which was broken with fear she faltered:

"Because . . . you are . . . known as the . . . 'Gentlemen of the Road,' and no . . . gentleman would . . . strike an . . . unarmed and helpless . . . man"

The highwayman looked at her, his eyes gleaming through the slits of his mask.

He chuckled and remarked:

"Ye've got courage, lidy, O'll say that for ye! Very well then! But tell His Nibs to keep 'is breakteeth curses to 'imself!"

Lord Rothwyn would have said something but quickly, even as the words came to his lips, Lalitha put her hand over his mouth.

She was well aware that he was in a rage when it would be hard for him to restrain himself whatever the consquences might be.

Then as he felt her thin fingers trembling against his lips he said in a low, controlled voice:

"I will not provoke him."

"Please do . . . not," Lalitha begged. "I'm so . . . frightened!"

He looked at her but he did not speak and she sat down again beside him, her breath coming quickly, her heart beating tumultuously.

She clasped both her hands round Lord Rothwyn's arm, to hold on to him to give her courage and a sense of protection.

The two highwaymen who had been in front of them led the team of chestnuts off the roadway and up a rough path into the wood.

They proceeded some way, leading both their own horses and the chestnuts until they came to a clearing where the trees had recently been felled.

Here they brought the horses to a stand-still and started to take them from the shafts.

The other highwayman, who had shot Lord Rothwyn, dragged Ned from the back of the curricule and tied him to a tree.

" 'ere, what're ye a-doing this for?" Ned asked.

"We dinna want ye a-lopping after us too quick like," the highwayman answered, "but I reckons ye'll 'ave yer hands full with a wounded man an' a woman ter look after!"

The fourth man was supervising the release of the horses. The highwayman who had tied up Ned walked to the side of the curricule.

"Yer purses," he ordered, "and everythin' else o' value, an' be sharp about it!"

As he spoke he bent forward and drew the pistol from the side-pocket where Lord Rothwyn had tried to reach it.

He turned it over in his hands and smiled.

"Better than Oi can afford!" he said. "Just as yer 'orses be better blood-stock than us 'ave th' pleasure o'."

He was, Lalitha knew, being deliberately provocative and her hands tightened on Lord Rothwyns' arm.

"Give the 'Gentleman of the Road' my purse!" Lord Rothwyn said in a calm but sarcastic voice.

Lalitha did as she was told and the highwayman's eyes fell on her ridicule.

"Oi might as well take that!" he said. " 't'll make a welcome gift for a wench Oi fancy!"

Lalitha handed it to him.

He took it, opened the purse, and gave a little whistle of surprise as he saw what was inside it.

"Generous 't yer be 'e?" he asked mockingly, with a side-long jerk of his head towards Lord Rothwyn. "In which case, gentleman or no gentleman, yer'll not wish t' accompany Oi?"

"No, thank you," Lalitha answered, "I have no wish to be hounded, hunted, and live in terror of being caught."

The highwayman laughed.

"Ye've got spirit!" he said. "Oi likes a woman with spirit!"

He looked at Lalitha, his eyes narrowed evilly, and there was a twist on his lips which frightened her.

She suddenly felt desperately afraid of something which she did not understand and she shrank back against Lord Rothwyn.

The highwayman put out his hand towards her and she felt Lord Rothwyn go tense.

Then there was a shout from the men who had been unfastening the horses.

They were free now and each highwayman was riding his own horse and leading one of His Lordship's by the bridle.

There was one still unattended. The highwayman dropped her arm.

"There be no time!" he said as he pushed Lord Rothwyn's pistol into his belt. "Pity! Ye're a pretty piece!"

He mounted his horse and rode to join the others.

He took the spare horse by the bridle and then so quickly it seemed incredible they disappeared amongst the trees.

Even as they went it began to rain.

Lalitha looked at Lord Rothwyn.

"I will see to your arm," she said, "but first we had best get under cover. Do you think you could walk to the shelter of the trees?"

"Yes, of course," he answered.

She saw with consternation that the side of his coat was soaked crimson with the blood from the wound and there was a tight look round his mouth.

She got out of the curricule and hurried round it to help him alight.

But he managed without her and walked quite steadily towards the trees.

Lalitha turned to Ned.

"I will come and release you in a moment," she told him. "I must first find somewhere for His Lordship to sit without getting wet."

"Oi be all right, M'Lady," Ned answered.

As they moved to where the trees were thick and the branches would prevent the worst of the rain beating down on them, Lalitha gave a little cry.

Immediately ahead was a wooden hut roughly made of split tree trunks.

It had obviously been put up by the wood-cutters who must have been working in this part of the forest.

She ran ahead, opened the door, and felt a wave of hot air.

There were only a few red ashes left in what was a roughly improvised fire-place but there had been a fire there perhaps only a few hours earlier.

She left the door open and ran back to Lord Rothwyn, who was moving slowly and slightly unsteadily through the trees.

"I have found a hut where we can shelter," she said breathlessly.

"That is a relief" he replied, but she knew that he spoke with an effort.

She helped him in through the door, which was so low that he had to bow his head, and he sank down on the sandy floor as if exhausted.

When she'd left the curricule Lalitha had carried with her the small bundle of possessions she had brought from Roth Park.

Now she opened it, saying:

"I am going to cut the sleeve away from your coat so that I can bandage your arm. I will try not to hurt you and it will be impossible to get your coat off without it being extremely painful."

"Thank you," Lord Rothwyn replied.

Lalitha had only her embroidery scissors, which were not large, but somehow she managed to cut through the super-fine cloth of Lord Rothwyn's superbly tailored coat and remove the sleeve.

She then had to cut away more of the shoulder, to find that the wound was almost at the top of his arm.

She thought, although she was not sure, that the bullet had passed through the flesh and had not shattered the bone.

But there was too much blood for her to be certain of anything.

It dripped down Lord Rothwyn's arm, ran down his side, and seemed to cover everything, including her hands, with a sticky crimson tide.

Finally when the wound was fully exposed Lalitha made a thick pad of the lawn and silk under-clothes that she had packed in her bundle.

She pressed it into place to staunch the flow of blood and bandaged it with her night-gown after she had torn it into strips.

By the time she had finished she could see even in the dim darkness of the hut that Lord Rothwyn was very pale, and she knew that he must be suffering considerable pain.

"I must now go and release Ned," she said.

"There is a flask of brandy in the curricule," Lord Rothwyn said. "Will you be kind enough to bring it to me."

"But of course," she answered. "Why did you not say so before?"

She ran as quickly as she could to be curricule.

By this time it was raining hard.

She snatched up the brandy and also the rug which had covered her gown and hurried back to the hut.

She opened the flask, gave it into Lord Rothwyn's hand, and picking up her scissors went to Ned.

It was quite a job to hack through the thick rope which the highwayman had used to bind him to the tree.

She tried first to untie the knot, but she found it was beyond the strength of her fingers.

"Oi'll get 'elp, M'Lady," Ned said when at last he was free.

"Yes, please do," Lalitha answered. "I am afraid it is quite a long way back to the last village. We seem to have passed it a long time ago."

"Oi may 'ave t' go further than that, M'Lady," Ned answered. "Those small hamlets are not likely to 'ave any sort of conveyance in which we could get His Lordship 'ome."

"No, I suppose not," Lalitha said with a sigh. "In which case, Ned, could we not take the cushions from the curricule into the hut to make His Lordship more comfortable? There has been a fire there."

"Oi'll re-light it for ye, M'Lady," Ned said. "At least you'll be warm and 'll be able to see while Oi am away."

He pulled the cushions from the curricule, carried them to the hut, and helped Lalitha arrange them so that Lord Rothwyn could sit on one and lean back against another.

By this time it was almost impossible to see until Ned got the fire alight.

Fortunately there were great stacks of logs just outside. Also, the wood-cutters, experienced in making themselves at home under any circumstances, had arranged a kind of rough chimney in the roof, which drew away the smoke.

'Oi'll be off now, M'Lord," Ned said. "Oi'll be as quick as Oi can."

"Thank you, Ned," Lord Rothwyn answered.

He was looking better, Lalitha thought, since he had drunk some brandy.

As she replaced the top of the flask she was thankful that the highwayman had not noticed it in the pocket with the pistol.

Ned disappeared into the darkness outside, having first brought in a pile of logs which Lalitha reckoned should last them for several hours.

She sat down on a cushion.

Noticing that Lord Rothwyn was holding his wounded arm in a somewhat uncomfortable manner, she gave an exclamation and rising went out of the hut.

A few seconds later she was back again, carrying in her hand her petticoat, which she had removed outside.

She laid it out on the ground and with her scissors cut out a sling.

Very gently she tied it round Lord Rothwyn's neck so that it supported his elbow.

"Is that better?" she asked.

"I can see you are a very competent Nurse!"

"I am only praying I have done the right thing," Lalitha answered. "Mama was so good at bandaging. They always sent for her if anyone was injured in the village, especially the children. But while I have helped her I have never had to do it all by myself before."

"I am very grateful."

She looked at him a little uncertainly and said in a low voice:

"It is all my . . . fault that this has . . . happened to you. How can I ever . . . pay you back for the . . . loss of your horses?"

"We might have lost worse things!" Lord Rothwyn replied dryly.

She thought that he was referring to the fact that the highwayman might have killed him.

Then she remembered her sudden fear as the highway man had put out his hand towards her and felt herself tremble.

"It is all right!" Lord Rothwyn said quietly, as if he read her thoughts. "It is all over now. We only have to endure a long wait until Ned brings help. I suggest you sit closer to me and the rag can cover us both."

"Yes, of course," Lalitha agreed. "That would be sensible."

She moved her cushion and could not help a little thrill that passed through her because she could feel his body against hers.

She was with him, touching him, and she had thought only a short time ago that she would never see him again!

She felt a little paean of thanks giving rise in her heart.

"I am afraid we shall miss our dinner!" Lord Rothwyn said. "And it was to be a very special occasion!"

"I am very . . . happy as it is," Lalitha answered.

"You were extremely brave," Lord Rothwyn remarked in a low voice, "and because I am afraid all this this will have over-tired you, I want you to drink a little brandy."

Lalitha was about to expostulate that she did not like brandy, but then she thought that it would be a mistake to argue.

He was wounded and she must do as he wanted. She also thought that his arm might be hurting him, and therefore it might be a good idea for him to have another drink.

She took several small sips from the flask and felt the brandy burn its way down through her body.

It dispelled the last little quivering feeling of fear that had not dispersed even when the highwaymen went away.

She knew when she began to think about it that she was still shocked from that moment of terror when she had seen Lord Rothwyn shot.

She handed him the flask.

He drank quiet an appreciable amount of what brandy was left, and she screwed the top back onto the bottle.

"Are you warmer?" he asked.

"I am . . . quite . . . all right. It is . . . you we must . . . worry . . . about."

She rose to put a few more logs on the fire, and when she re-joined him she saw that he had slipped a little further down against the cushions so that he no longer had to hold his head upright.

"The most sensible thing we could do," he said in a tired voice, "would be to try to get some sleep."

"Let us try to do that," Lalitha agreed.

He yawned and she knew that it was the reaction of what he had passed through, and also he had lost a lot of blood.

He shut his eyes and she turned her head to look at him in the light of the fire.

He was so incredibly handsome! she thought. She was here alone with him and did not have to say good-bye to him forever.

What had happened? What had he said to Sophie and why had he followed her?

There were a dozen questions to which she wanted the answers, but she knew that this was not the moment to ask them.

All she could do now was to be content with what the gods had given back to her.

The man she loved was beside her and whatever the future held, she could be with him for at least a little while longer.

"I love you!" she wanted to say aloud.

Instead she said it in her heart over and over again! 'I love you! I love you!'

Chapter Six

Lalitha was awakened by a house-maid coming quietly into the room to pull back the curtains.

Without moving she lay for a moment watching the golden glow of the sun-shine spread over the ceiling and envelop the whole room.

The maid was followed by Nattie, bringing in a collar and lead for Royal so that he could be taken for a walk in the garden.

It was over a week, Lalitha thought, since they had come back to London.

When Ned had finally brought a conveyance, it had been a shorter journey for them to Rothwyn House than back to the country, and also, Lalitha knew, it was important for Lord Rothwyn to see a Surgeon immediately.

It had been dawn before she had heard foot-steps coming through the wood towards the hut.

Lord Rothwyn was asleep and very gently so as not to startle him she said quietly:

"Ned has returned."

He opened his eyes and realised that Lalitha held him in her arms and his head was against her breast.

At first when he had suggested that they both should go to sleep he had relaxed with his head back against the cushions brought in from the curricule.

It did not look very comfortable but at least his injured arm was free of all contact which could have hurt it.

As Lalitha lay awake beside him, thinking of him and of her love for him, he became a little restless.

He murmured in his sleep and she guessed that his wound was hurting him and he might have a fever.

She did not know what to do, but sat as near as possible watching him in the light of the fire for fear he should move about roughly so that he would start his wound bleeding again.

Then unexpectedly slipping still lower against the cushions, he had turned towards her. Automatically her arms went round him.

He put his head against her breast and, as if that was what he had been seeking, fell into a deep slumber.

At first she was too frightened to move, almost to breathe, but then the feeling of him so close against her awakened a strange sensation she had never known before.

She loved him desperately but what she now felt was not only love for a man who was strong and masculine, as she had already told herself, out of reach.

It was also a love that had something protective, compassionate, and maternal in it.

She wanted to save Lord Rothwyn from all that was unpleasant, harsh, and evil in life.

For the moment she felt as if he were a child whom she must defend against unhappiness, misery, and loneliness.

Her arms tightened round him and now by just bending her head a little she could touch his hair with her lips.

It was soft and silky and as she kissed it she felt ashamed of her own daring.

But he would never know, she thought, and when he was no longer interested in her she would always have this moment to remember, when she could feel the nearness of his head against her breast and he had turned to her as if seeking something which only she could give him.

She did not sleep and although her arm became numb and cramped she did not move.

She knew that this was an ecstasy and a wonder that

she had never known before and which in some strange manner made up for all she had suffered in the past years.

This was something no-one, not even Sophie, could take away from her and for the rest of her life she would treasure it in her heart.

When Lord Rothwyn awakened he realised how he was lying and for a moment he did not move, but just as Ned reached the door of the hut he straightened himself.

Without looking at him Lalitha moved away from his side, conscious that her arm was very painful, yet she forced herself to speak quite naturally as she asked:

"You have brought a carriage with you, Ned?"

"A comfortable one, M'Lady!"

"That is good!"

"Help me to my feet, Ned," Lord Rothwyn commanded.

As the groom hastened to obey him Lalitha, pulling her cloak around her shoulders, walked ahead to where the carriage was waiting.

They drove the few miles to London almost in silence.

When they reached Rothwyn House Lord Rothwyn was helped upstairs and Lalitha, because she was concerned only with his health, asked that a groom go at once in search of a Surgeon.

"His Lordship employs Mr. Henry Clive, My Lady," the Major-Domo informed her. "He is one of the Specialists who attends His Royal Highness."

"Then ask him to come here as quickly as possible," Lalitha said. "Who is His Lordship's Physician?"

"That will be Sir William Knighton," the Major-Domo answered, "one of his Royal Highness's Physicians-in-Ordinary."

They had both been sent for and only after she had heard their report on His Lordship did Lalitha, tired and exhausted, go to bed.

She slept until late in the afternoon and when she awoke it was to find that Nattie had arrived from Roth Park, bringing Royal with her.

She had been delighted to see them and Nattie had immediately with unchangeable authority made rules and regulations which Lalitha was forced to keep.

Despite all her protests she had been made to stay in bed for three days and then only been allowed to take a short walk in the gardens surrounding Rothwyn House.

Afterwards she was allowed to read and occupy herself with nothing more strenuous than putting together the poem written by Lord Hadley.

"I am well! I am quite well, Nattie!" Lalitha had protested.

"There's two opinions on that!" Nattie replied darkly.

Although Lalitha would not admit it, she did feel weak and listless.

"It was the shock of seeing Lord Rothwyn shot," she told herself.

But it was also, although she tried to forget it, the misery and sense of despair she had endured when Sophie had forced her away, into what was to have been obscurity.

Now she was back at Rothwyn House, but at the same time her pleasure was in some ways spoilt because she could not see Lord Rothwyn.

She hoped and expected that he would send for her, but the days passed and although Nattie told her how he was getting on, he did not invite her to go to his room.

At last shyly she asked Nattie:

"Could I not . . . see His Lordship?"

"Sir William said His Lordship was to have no visitors for the first two days," Nattie replied, "and since then he has not asked for Your Ladyship."

Lalitha hesitated and then she said:

"I would like to see him. Why does he not . . . wish to see me?"

Nattie smiled.

"I think all men, M'Lady, and perhaps Master Inigo more than others, feel ashamed when they're laid low. He was always the same even when he was small. He would not admit he felt ill or in pain. Many's the time I've said to him: 'You might be an animal for all you tell me about yourself!' "

Lalitha gave a little laugh.

"And what did he reply to that?"

"He would not talk about weakness," Nattie replied. "Once when he was really ill and he didn't hear me coming into the Night-Nursery he was repeating to himself over and over again: 'I am well! I am well! I am well!' "

Lalitha remembered how brave Lord Rothwyn had been about his wounded arm although it must have been very painful.

So it was comforting in some way to think that he did not wish to see her for a reason which amounted to conceit, rather than the fact that he felt no need of her presence.

At the same time she yearned for him.

Now because she could not prevent herself as Lalitha sat up against her pillows she asked:

"How is His Lordship this morning?"

"I've not seen him," Nattie replied, "but from the size of the breakfast being carried into his room as I came down the passage I imagine he's fit as a fiddle!"

Lalitha laughed.

"You told me yesterday that the wound has nearly healed."

"Mr. Clive is very pleased with His Lordship's progress," Nattie answered. "He says he has never known a gentleman to heal so quickly or so cleanly."

"I am . . . glad of that!" Lalitha said a little breathlessly.

Nattie did not answer and after a moment she went on:

"It is a lovely day! I want to get up and go into the garden with Royal."

"Then keep him away from the flower-beds," Nattie admonished. "If you'd heard what the gardeners had to say about the mess he made it'd make Your Ladyship's ears tingle!"

"He was very naughty!" Lalitha admitted. "He was quite convinced there was a bone buried under the geraniums!"

Because she thought that Royal's behaviour might amuse Lord Rothwyn she had drawn a little pencil sketch of the small dog digging up flowers and kicking the soil all over the smooth, green lawn.

She put it in an envelope and asked Nattie to take it to His Lordship.

When she heard that it had made him laugh, she drew another sketch of a closed door with the dogs and herself waiting patiently outside as if longing to go for a walk.

She had never been any use at painting with water-colours, which was considered an important part of every young lady's accomplishments, but she could draw little cartoons which had often amused her father.

It had given her a feeling of satisfaction to send her efforts to Lord Rothwyn merely because she longed to communicate with him in one way or another.

She even dared to hope that perhaps he would send her a note in return, but she was disappointed.

Perhaps, she thought in sudden fear, he was already regretting that he had prevented her from disappearing as she had meant to do into the wilds of Norfolk.

Perhaps now he thought he had made a mistake and was no longer interested in her! Then she remembered how he had said that he never left unfinished a building on which he was working.

She was certainly not finished as yet, but when she was . . .

It was like a dark cloud on the horizon to remember that someday that would happen and then perhaps she would have to leave him.

She took Royal into the garden, and because she played with him, throwing him a stick and then a small ball, he behaved with propriety.

Lalitha had luncheon alone and when she went up-stairs to rest on Nattie's strict instructions she found the Nurse waiting in her bed-room.

"I hope you're going to try and sleep, M'Lady, and not wear yourself out reading those books," Nattie said as she saw what Lalitha was carrying.

"I want to read for a little while," she replied pleadingly.

"Well, not for too long," Nattie said firmly. "You have to look your best tonight."

"To . . . night?"

"His Lordship has asked if you will dine with him."

"Oh, Nattie!"

Lalitha could harly breathe the words.

After a moment she managed to say:

"His Lordship has . . . recovered?"

"I understand, M'Lady, we shall all be returning to Roth Park tomorrow."

"Oh, I am glad . . . so very . . . glad!" Lalitha cried.

She felt as if someone had taken all the sun-shine from the sky and put it into her arms; she felt as if she could dance on air or fly to the moon!

He was better! He wanted to see her and they were to dine together!

Because she wished so desperately to look her best for him, she did sleep for a little while, then lay awake counting the minutes until it was time to dress for dinner.

As she bathed, Nattie brought from the wardrobe a gown she had never seen before.

"His Lordship wishes you to wear this tonight."

It was quite different from any dress Lalitha had imagined herself wearing.

She was not even certain of the colour.

There seemed to be layers of gauze in shades of blue and green over a silver foundation.

It was soft and indeterminate and while it revealed the soft curves of her figure it made her look very ethereal.

As Lalitha stared at herself in the mirror Nattie brought a large leather box and set it down on the dressing-table.

"His Lordship asked if you would wear these."

She opened the box and Lalitha saw that it contained a necklace of tiny diamond stars exquisitely set and so delicate that they might have been fashioned by fairy fingers.

Nattie fastened the necklace and then there were several stars to match to be arranged in her hair.

The diamonds seemed to pick up the new lights which had become more prominent day after day.

Now her hair no longer felt limp and lank but waved with a buoyancy when it fell over her shoulders and had a thickness and a sheen which had never been there before.

It was due, Lalitha knew, to the peach lotion which Nattie applied every night, on the Herb-Woman's instructions, and she had learnt also that hair quicker than anything else revealed the health of the body.

There was also a bracelet of stars in the box which matched the necklace and Lalitha put it on.

She rose from the dressing-table to stand looking at herself in a long mirror in which she was reflected from the top of her glittering head to the small, buckle-trimmed slippers which matched her gown.

It was hard to recognise the miserable, thin, frightened girl whom Lord Rothwyn had married in a desire for revenge.

For a moment Lalitha could only see her own eyes shining like the stars in the softness of her hair.

She could see too that her skin was white and clear, that her neck was soft and rounded and there were no 'salt-cellars' as the base of it as there had been before.

"You look lovely, M'Lady!"

Then even as Lalitha flushed a little at the compliment she saw instead of her own face, Sophie's exquisite, breath-takingly beautiful countenace, with her blue eyes, gold hair, and pink and white skin.

She turned away from the mirror.

It was useless, she thought, to hope that Lord Rothwyn might admire her as he had Sophie, but perhaps he would still be kind to her out of . . . pity.

But whatever he might feel about her, she still loved him and she wanted to see him so urgently that it was with the greatest difficulty that she forced herself not to run but to walk down the staircase to the Salon.

She had thought of him every minute during the past week and yet when she saw him again she did not remembered how overwhelmingly handsome and elegant he was.

He was waiting for her at the end of the Salon and as she walked towards him she knew that no man could look so magnificent and so irresistible.

His evening-coat fitted him like a second skin and his white cravat was a masterpiece of intricacy beneath the high points of his collar.

His skin did not look quite so sun-burnt and he was also a trifle thinner, but it actually made him even more attractive than he had been before.

Lalitha drew nearer to him, her eyes on his, and as she was trying to find the words to tell him how glad she was that he had recovered he exclaimed:

"At last I know the colour of your hair!"

She looked up at him enquiringly and he went on:

"I could never put a name to it before but it is moon-light on water!"

For a moment Lalitha was too surprised even to blush. Then as the colour came to her cheeks Lord Rothwyn raised her hand to his lips.

"Forgive me!" he said, "I should have said first how delighted I am to see you!"

"You have recovered?" she asked in a low voice.

"They tell me I have been an exemplary patient!"

She longed to ask him why she had not been allowed to see him, but before she could formulate the words he went on:

"The rest has done you good. That is what I wanted. You look different in every way and I am sure you have put on a little weight."

"A lot of weight!" Lalitha answered with laughter in her voice. "Nearly four pounds!"

"I congratulate you!"

She had the strange feeling that while their lips were saying one thing their minds were saying something else.

She found it hard to look into his eyes.

At the same time she felt strange little thrills of happiness running through her like quicksilver.

It was hard to speak, hard to breathe, and she could not help remembering how heavy Lord Rothwyn's head had felt against her breasts.

"We have a great many things to talk about," he

said, and then before he could begin the Butler announced that dinner was served.

What they ate or what they drank Lalitha had no idea.

She only knew that it was an excitement and a joy that she had never known before to sit beside him and listen to his voice.

The table was decorated with green orchids and as course succeeded course served on crested, silver dishes by quiet, well-trained servants in their colourful livery, Lalitha kept feeling that she must be dreaming.

Could she really be the same girl who had cooked herself something to eat when she had time and when there was anything in the house, and who ate at the kitchen table because her Step-mother would not allow her to sit down in the Dining-Room?

After dinner when they returned to the Salon Lord Rothwyn said.

"I knew that jewellery would become you. It belonged to my mother. She always told me when she was young it was her favourite."

"It is very lovely!" Lalitha said, "and it is kind of you to lend it to me."

"It is a gift!" Lord Rothwyn said quietly.

She looked up at him in astonishment and he added:

"I have another present for you as well."

"But you . . . s-should not . . . I m-mean . . . you c-cannot . . . m-mean it," Lalitha stammered.

"I would wish to repay you for your care of my wound," Lord Rothwyn said, "and what is more I have the feeling that if you had not protected me from the highwaymen my injuries might have been far worse than they were."

He saw Lalitha give a shudder as she remembered how the highwayman had turned his pistol, ready to strike Lord Rothwyn on the head.

He said quickly:

"But there is no reason now to talk of it. We have so many other things to discuss."

Because he spoke so authoritatively Lalitha tried to force the memory of what had happened from her mind, and she said a little shyly:

"I do not . . . know how to . . . thank . . . you. But I have a . . . present for . . . you."

"For me?" Lord Rothwyn asked in surprise.

"It is not a valuable one," Lalitha answered, "but I do hope it will please you."

She crossed the room to the *secretaire* at which she had sat in the afternoons during the past week.

She took a piece of paper from a drawer.

"I have pieced together Lord Hadley's poem," she said, "and I have only had to guess a few words, which were not important."

"Will you read it to me?" Lord Rothwyn asked.

Lalitha opened the paper which she held in her hand, then in her soft voice read:

> "The call of the heart is the call of love
> But I swear by Heaven above
> Now and forever my love is true
> If your heart calls my heart to you."

As she finished she looked up at Lord Rothwyn for his approval.

"It was very clever of you to re-construct it," he said, "and Lord Hadley expresses himself most eloquently."

"He may not have been the Lord Byron of his day," Lalitha smiled, "but I imagine how thrilled the lady in question would have been to receive his poem."

"Do you think that her heart called to his?"

Lord Rothwyn's voice was deep and the question seemed to Lalitha to be almost a personal one.

She did not know why but she found it hard to reply, and then in another tone he said:

"Now let me give you another present which is a *quid pro quo* for those delightful sketches you drew for me."

"I thought they might . . . amuse you."

"They did!" Lord Rothwyn replied, "and although what I have for you will not make you laugh, I think they will please you."

He took a small portfolio from the table which

stood beside his chair, which Lalitha had not noticed before, and put it into her hands.

When she untied the ribbon with which it was tied she found inside there were three pencil drawings.

She looked at one for a moment and her eyes widened in astonishment.

"That is by Michaelangelo," Lord Rothwyn said. "It is called *The Running Youth*."

"It is beautiful! Unbelievably beautiful!" Lalitha said in awe-struck tones.

She turned to the next and saw that it was a landscape filled with detail; a panoramic vision at which she felt she could go on looking for hours.

"That one is drawn by Pieter Brueghel," Lord Rothwyn told her, "and the last is the one I think you will like the best."

It was the head of an angel and the spiritual, mystical look on her face made Lalitha feel that at last she knew what real beauty should look like.

"It is by Leonardo Da Vinci," Lord Rothwyn explained. "It was one of his first sketches for the angel in the picture called *The Virgin on the Rocks*."

"Are these . . . really for . . . me?" Lalitha asked almost beneath her breath. "I cannot . . . believe it!"

"I want you to answer me a question," Lord Rothwyn said. "Look at the picture over the mantel-piece."

Lalitha looked up as he told her to do.

She saw that the picture was by Rubens and must be very valuable. The vivid colours and the brilliant outline of the figure were awe-inspiring.

"Now tell me," Lord Rothwyn went on, "which means the more to you, the finished painting by Rubens, acclaimed master of his craft, or the drawings that you hold in your hand?"

Lalitha thought for a moment and then she said:

"Both are wonderful in their way. Both give me a feeling of inexpressible beauty, but . . ."

She paused.

"Go on," Lord Rothwyn prompted.

"Perhaps it is only a personal feeling," Lalitha said, "but to me these sketches are more . . . inspiring."

Lord Rothwyn smiled.

"Did you know that William Blake, who was a friend of mine and is of course both an artist and a poet, said once: 'Not drawing—but inspiration!' "

"No, I did not know that," Lalitha answered. "It is what . . . happens to me when I look at them . . . what happens . . . inside me."

She felt that she had not explained herself very well and went on:

"I feel as if I do not look at a drawing with my . . . eyes but with my . . . soul."

Feeling that she had perhaps sounded too emotional, she said:

"You will . . . laugh at me for being . . . sentimental!"

"I am not laughing, Lalitha," Lord Rothwyn said. "I want to tell you something."

He put out his hand towards her as he spoke and covered hers.

She was not certain whether it was the touch of his fingers or the note in his voice that made her feel as if she could not move, and that something strange and very wonderful was about to happen.

Almost as though he compelled her to do so she raised her eyes to his and was spell-bound.

He was looking at her in a way which he had never looked at her before; in a manner which no man had ever looked at her. It seemed to take the very breath from her body.

"Lalitha!" Lord Rothwyn exclaimed.

Behind them the door opened.

"Sir William Knighton, M'Lord," the Major-Domo announced.

For a moment it seemed to Lalitha as if the interruption did not reach their minds and they could not comprehend what had happened.

Lord Rothwyn held her to him by a spell that was inescapable.

Then, as if he broke a thread which bound them irrevocably to each other, he took his hand from hers and rose to his feet.

"Sir William!" he exclaimed. "I was not expecting you."

"No, indeed, My Lord, and I had intended to call in the morning before you left for the country."

Sir William Knighton had by this time reached Lord Rothwyn and the two men shook hands.

A quiet, unobtrusive, middle-aged man, industrious, conscientious, and discreet, Sir William, besides being His Royal Highness's Physician, had recently become a close confidant of the Regent.

"You must forgive my intrusion at this late hour," Sir William continued, "but His Royal Highness has requested that I should attend him in Brighton tomorrow and I must therefore make an early start."

"Of course I understand," Lord Rothwyn said.

"I thought therefore instead of inconveniencing you by calling before breakfast," Sir William said, "I would look at your shoulder this evening, and then Your Lordship can return to the country without further anxiety."

"That is very obliging of you," Lord Rothwyn said, and added:

"I do not think, Sir William, that you have met my wife?"

"Your wife?" Sir William ejaculated as he bowed.

There was no doubt of the surprise in his eyes.

"Our marriage has been kept a secret," Lord Rothwyn explained, "and I should be grateful if you would not mention it to His Royal Highness until he receives a letter from me."

"I will respect your confidence," Sir William answered. "As Your Lordship is well aware, I am discretion itself!"

Lord Rothwyn smiled.

"We both know that the Regent is very angered if he does not learn of anything closely concerning his friends before anyone else."

"That is true," Sir William agreed and his eyes were twinkling.

"We must not keep you, I am sure you are very busy," Lord Rothwyn said. "Shall we repair to my bed-room?"

"Of course, My Lord," Sir William agreed.

It seemed to Lalitha that Lord Rothwyn hesitated a moment and then he said:

"In which case, Lalitha, it would be best if we say good-night to each other. I would not wish to keep you up late when we have a tiring day ahead of us. We leave at noon, if that suits you."

"I will be ready," Lalitha answered.

Lord Rothwyn raised her hand to his lips.

She thought for a moment, although afterwards she was certain that she had imagined it, that his mouth lingered for a moment against the softness of her skin.

Then, leading the way with Sir William following him, Lord Rothwyn left the Salon and she heard them going upstairs.

She was disappointed! She felt like a child who having being taken to a Pantomime finds the curtain falls unexpectedly and without a satisfactory ending.

Sensibly she told herself there was tomorrow and they were going back to Roth Park.

They would be together. She would drive there with Lord Rothwyn and their conversation could continue from where it had been interrupted.

She opened her portfolio.

How could he have given her anything so beautiful, so exquisite?

She knew that such drawings must have cost a great deal of money.

That was immaterial. What was important was that he had found something that was exactly to her taste.

They were "an inspiration." Did he think that she needed inspiring?

She had the feeling that he was trying to tell her something and the drawings were part of a message he wished to convey to her.

She looked again at the head of the angel. There was something about it which made her thrill in some way as when his lips had touched her hand.

How did he know? How did he guess that the drawings could move her far more than paintings and she had always longed to possess one?

She felt that there was so much she wanted to say to him; so much she wanted to hear.

Almost automatically she tidied the cushions on the sofa. She had been forced to do it so often in her Stepmother's house.

Then as she took up the portfolio preparatory to going up to her own room she realised that the piece of paper on which she had written Lord Hadley's poem was no longer there.

Lord Rothwyn must have taken it with him.

Was he pleased with her efforts?

There was so much more she wanted to tell him about the difficulty of putting together the pieces.

The words that she could not find, but which she had fitted in, to make sense of what the writer had written all those centuries ago.

Slowly Lalitha went up the stairs.

It had been a wonderful evening and yet she could not help feeling that it might have been even more wonderful if Sir William had not interrupted them.

What had Lord Rothwyn been going to say to her?

She did not dare to guess.

She reached her bed-room to find not Nattie, as she had expected, or Robinson, the older house-maid who usually attended her, but a much younger girl. Lalitha remembered her name.

"Good-evening, Elsie," she said. "Where is Nattie?"

"Nurse was not feeling well, M'Lady, nor Miss Robinson either."

"Not well?" Lalitha asked.

"I think it was something they ate for supper, M'Lady. They've both been taken sick and so I said I would look after you."

"I do hope Nattie will be all right," Lalitha said. "Shall I go up and see her?"

"I think she would rather be left alone, M'Lady. No-one wants to see people when they're being sick."

"No, I suppose not," Lalitha agreed, "but the Doctor is here. He could see Nurse if it was serious."

"Oh no, M'Lady!" Elsie answered soothingly, "it's not as bad as all that. I think perhaps the fish was not as fresh as it might have been, and both Nurse and Miss Robinson say they have squeamish stomachs. I am all right and I ate from the same dish."

"Then perhaps they are not too bad," Lalitha smiled.

She walked across to the dressing-table to unclasp the diamond necklace.

Lord Rothwyn could not have really intended it as a gift, she thought.

Perhaps she had not heard him aright. Perhaps he had only meant a gift for the time she was at Roth Park.

She felt as if she could not think clearly and remember exactly what he had said.

She had been so conscious of him; of being so close to him; of being affected by the deep note in his voice.

She put the diamond stars in her hair back into the box and then the bracelet.

As she did so there came a knock at the door.

"I expect that will be Royal," she said to Elsie.

Royal had been taken by one of the footmen for a walk after they left the Dining-Room.

She thought now that he had been away a long time.

Usually he was let into the Salon, or wherever she might be, not more than a quarter of an hour after he had been collected.

Elsie went to the door.

She spoke to someone outside and then came back to Lalitha's side.

"I'm afraid, M'Lady, that Royal has been in an accident!"

"An accident?" Lalitha said sharply. "Where? What has happened?"

"It's not serious, M'Lady, but will you see him?"

"Yes, yes of course," Lalitha said. "Where is he?"

"Follow me, M'Lady," Elsie said.

She went ahead of Lalitha, who followed her not down the main staircase but along the passage and down another flight of stairs which she knew led to the side of the house.

It was the quickest way to the garden, Lalitha thought, and she hurried after Elsie, who was moving very swiftly, feeling anxious.

She loved Royal and she knew how much he loved her.

She had grown used to him being always beside her,

sleeping on her bed at night although Nattie said he
should keep to his basket. Wherever she went he was
there behind her, a little shadow at her heels.

How could anything have happened to him? Lalitha
wondered.

The footmen always kept him on a lead when they
took him for a walk first thing in the morning or last
thing at night.

It was only when Royal was with her that he was
allowed to roam loose because she knew he would come
to her the moment she called him.

Elsie was now leading her along a corridor in a
part of the house where she had never been before.

There appeared to be no-one about and she guessed
that most of the servants would have gone to bed with
the exception of the footman in the main Hall.

At last ahead of them was a side door and Elsie
pulled it open.

There was a carriage outside.

Lalitha realised that it was standing at the side of
the house which further round led to the kitchen entrance.

'Royal must have been run over!' she thought with a
feeling of horror.

There was a footman standing beside the carriage-
door.

"Royal is inside, M'Lady," Elsie said, and Lalitha
moved forward.

She looked inside the coach. It was dark. Then suddenly a cloth was thrown over her head.

As she gasped and tried to struggle she was dragged
forcibly inside the carriage and thrown roughly onto
the back seat.

She heard the door slam behind her and as it did
so the horses started moving.

For a moment Lalitha could hardly credit what was
happening.

She struggled with all her strength but the cloth over
her head was thick and now she felt rough hands
winding a cord round her. It held her arms straight at
her sides and pulled the cloth so that it was taut from
the top of her head to her waist.

"Help!" she tried to scream. "Help!"

The sound was stifled. Then a rough voice said:

"Make a noise and Oi'll give ye somewat that'll silence ye!"

It was a rough, uncouth voice, and Lalitha knew that the man who spoke meant what he said.

The fear of being hurt returned to her with all the fright and terror that she had known so often before.

It was impossible for her to make a sound; impossible after the man had spoken even to move; she could only lie as he had put her, in a corner of the carriage, completely helpless.

Now he was tying her ankles together and the rope was cutting into her skin and hurting her.

"That be better!" he said, "an' if Oi'ave so much as a chirp out o' ye until Oi say ye can speak Oi'll bash ye unconscious! Be that clear?"

Lalitha was far too afraid to answer.

She heard him give a chuckle as if of satisfaction. Then, having tied her legs together, he sat down on the seat beside her.

After a moment she knew by the smell of raw tobacco that he was smoking.

What was going to happen to her? Where was he taking her? And how did it concern Royal?

Then she knew that Royal had nothing to do with it.

He had not suffered an accident. He had merely been used as a decoy to get her from her bed-room and outside the house to where the carriage was waiting for her.

But why? What did it mean? Where was she being taken?

Then, insidiously, coming into her mind like the slithering of a revolting reptile, she knew the answer.

These were the people who Lord Rothwyn had told her spirited young women away and who were known as the "White Slave Traders."

Even as the thought came to her Lalitha cried out against it.

It could not be true. It must be a figment of her imagination.

She could not be involved in anything so horrible, so degrading, so terrifying!

But the idea persisted.

Where else would she be going? Who else would want her?

It could not be robbers, for she had already taken off her jewellry.

Besides, who would have known what she would be wearing this evening?

She thought of Elsie.

She had seemed a pleasant enough maid and yet she was not, Lalitha thought, exactly the type of simple country girl one might have expected to find in the London house of someone with a large country Estate.

Her mother had so often explained to her how the great Land-owners employed as servants in their household generation after generation of the same family.

They became knife-boy and then pantry-boy, footman, Butler, and Major-Domo in their turn.

First, second, and third scullery, kitchen, still-room maids, assistant-cook, and Cook; that was the ladder for the women.

Had Elsie risen from fifth or fourth house-maid to number two? Or had she lied when she said that only Nattie and Miss Robinson were ill because of what they had eaten for supper?

Was it a genuine illness or had it been contrived?

There were so many questions for which Lalitha could find no answers, but each one of them made her more afraid, more panic-stricken about what was happening to her and what lay ahead.

Then somehow she knew that if indeed it was the "White Slave Traders" who were taking her away to dispose of her so that no-one would ever see her again, there was someone else responsible for their action!

Who had planned exactly the manner in which she could be tricked into falling in with their scheme?

There was only one person who hated her to the point where she wished her dead, one person who wished to revenge herself because Sophie was not Lord Rothwyn's wife as she wished to be.

One woman—one person of whom she was more afraid than of anyone else in the whole world.

Her so-called Step-mother!

Chapter Seven

Lord Rothwyn stirred, feeling that someone had called him. He found himself listening, then he heard a dog whining.

He wondered where the animal could be, then heard a sharp bark followed again by continued whining, and realised that it was Royal.

It was coming from Lalitha's bed-room, which communicated with his but the door between them had not been opened since she'd come to Rothwyn House.

He listened for a little while longer and then decided that something must be wrong.

He was convinced that Royal would not whine in such a manner if Lalitha was with him, if she had been asleep as his bark would undoubtedly have awakened her.

Lord Rothwyn rose, lit the candle beside his bed, and put on his silk robe. Walking to the communicating door, he knocked on it gently.

The only reply was another sharp bark from Royal and after waiting for a moment he opened the door.

The room was in darkness and he went back to fetch the candle from beside his bed.

Royal followed him, jumped up at him eagerly, and now Lord Rothwyn was certain that something was amiss.

He returned to Lalitha's bed-room.

There was a faint, sweet fragrance on the air which he realised he always associated with her, but when he raised his candle high so that its light could illuminate the bed he saw that it had not been slept in.

For a moment he found it hard to think; impossible

to formulate in his own mind what could have happened.

Where had Lalitha gone? Why was she not here?

It was inconceivable at this late hour of the night that she should still be downstairs where he had left her when he'd said good-night and gone to his own bedroom with Sir William Knighton.

Urgently, aware of an acute feeling of apprehension, he went back into his own room and pulled violently at the bell-rope.

He jerked it up and down for several seconds, then opened the outer door and went out onto the landing.

The downstairs part of the house was in darkness. There was only the quiet ticking of the grandfather clock in the Hall.

What could have happened? How was it possible that Lalitha could have disappeared?

He turned towards his own bed-room, and as he did so his valet came running down the passage, buttoning his waistcoat, his hair dishevelled, and a look of apprehension on his face.

"What is it, M'Lord?" he asked. "Are you ill?"

"Where is Her Ladyship?" Lord Rothwyn demanded. "She is not in her bed-room."

"Not in her room, M'Lord?"

The valet glanced through the open communicating door as if he felt that His Lordship must be mistaken.

"She must be somewhere in the house," Lord Rothwyn said as if he wished to convince himself. "Go up to Nurse's room and see if she is there, if she is not, awaken the Major-Domo and tell him to come to me immediately."

"I'll do that, M'Lord."

The valet hurried away and Lord Rothwyn began to dress.

He looked at the clock and saw that it was just after two in the morning.

Could it be possible, he asked himself, that Lalitha had run away again?

He was sure that she had been glad when he had brought her back the last time after Sophie had driven her out of Roth Park.

He had seen the tears on her face and when she had come from the stage-coach to join him in the curricule, and he had known by her expression when she had joined him downstairs this evening in the Salon that she was happier than he had ever seen her before.

If she had gone away, then he was sure it was not of her own contriving. But who could have persuaded her once again to leave him?

"It is not possible!" he murmured to himself.

He was almost dressed when his valet came back into the room. Behind him was the Major-Domo.

"Nurse has not seen Her Ladyship, M,Lord," the valet said.

Lord Rothwyn turned to the Major-Domo.

"Hobson, have the house searched from top to bottom," he said, "and find out if anyone has seen Her Ladyship leave."

"I'll do that, M'Lord."

"No-one called after Sir William Knighton left?" Lord Rothwyn asked.

"No-one, M'Lord, while I was in the Hall, but I'll enquire of the footman who was on night-duty."

"Do that, and hurry," Lord Rothwyn said. "At the same time order a carriage. I may need one—I do not know."

The Major-Domo left and the valet assisted Lord Rothwyn into his coat.

He did not speak because he was thinking deeply, trying to imagine what could have happened, wondering where he should look for Lalitha.

Even if she had intended, for some strange reason of her own, to journey to Norfolk to her old Nurse, it would be unlikely that she would have left in the middle of the night.

She would be aware that there were no stage-coaches leaving London until six or seven o'clock in the morning, and had she wished to run away it would have been quite soon enough for her to leave the house at five.

"Did Nurse notice anything unusual about Her Ladyship when she put her to bed?" he asked at length.

"Nurse was taken ill last night, M'Lord, and so were the two head house-maids."

"Then who attended Her Ladyship?"

"I'm not certain, M'Lord, but I think it would have been Elsie."

"Fetch her here immediately!" Lord Rothwyn ordered.

The valet hurried to obey. Lord Rothwyn put some loose guineas into his trouser pocket and opened a wallet to see if, as he expected, there were a number of Bank-notes in it.

He had the feeling that he must be prepared, but for what he had no idea.

Royal was sitting on the hearth-rug watching him and he wondered what the dog knew and what he could tell if only he could talk.

For one thing, why had he been alone in Lalitha's bed-room?

If he had joined her downstairs; as was usual after his walk, would she have brought him upstairs and shut him in the room alone?

There were so many unanswerable questions.

He wondered if Lalitha had taken anything with her.

He remembered a cloak she had been wearing when she had travelled in the stage-coach.

It had been among the clothes he had ordered to be sent to Rothwyn House, and he remembered thinking that the very dark blue of the material made her skin seem dazzling white in contrast.

He walked once again into her bed-room and opened the wardrobe doors.

It was filled with gowns, some of which Nattie had brought back with her from Rothwyn House.

Others were new, of which he had approved the designs and which had been delivered since Lalitha had been in London.

He looked at them and realised two things: the dress Lalitha had been wearing tonight was not there, but the cloak which in fact was the only one she possessed was hanging by itself at one side of the wardrobe.

He walked to the dressing-table and then saw that the jewellery-case which contained the set of diamond stars which had belonged to his mother was lying open.

The necklace, the bracelet, and the stars that Lalitha

had worn in her hair had all been put back into the hollowed-out places into which they fitted.

Lord Rothwyn stared at them; then, hearing voices, he went back into his own room.

The door opened and the Major-Domo entered. With him were four servants.

"You have found out something, Hobson?" Lord Rothwyn asked quickly, as if he could not wait for the Major-Domo to speak first.

"I've discovered something very strange, M'Lord," the Major-Domo replied.

"What is it?"

"Henry here took the little dog Royal into the gardens tonight after dinner, as is usual, M'Lord."

"I meant no harm—I swear I meant no harm, M'Lord," Henry whimpered.

"Be silent!" the Major-Domo said sharply. "Let me tell His Lordship."

"Go on," Lord Rothwyn prompted.

"But Henry did not take the dog straight back to Her Ladyship, as was his orders," the Major-Domo continued. "Later in the evening George heard Royal whining and scratching at the door of an out-house."

Lord Rothwyn glanced at the young footman who he remembered was a nephew of the Butler at Roth Park.

"You were certain it was Royal?"

"I was certain, M'Lord, 'though I didn't see 'im."

"You did not open the door?"

"No, M'Lord, it was locked."

"Then how did you know it was Royal?"

"I've taken 'im out often enough, M'Lord, both 'ere and in the country. When I whistled to 'im 'e were quiet."

"What did you do about his being locked up?"

"I spoke to Henry, M'Lord," the Major-Domo replied.

"What did he say?"

"He said if I knew what was good for me I'd keep my mouth shut!"

"Go on," Lord Rothwyn said to the Major-Domo.

"I've also found, M'Lord," the Major-Domo continued, "that Nurse, Miss Robinson, the first house-maid, and Rose, the second house-maid were all taken ill after supper this evening. Elsie therefore waited on Her Ladyship."

Lord Rothwyn glanced at Elsie.

She was wearing a white shawl over her flannel night-gown and her hair fell untidily on either side of her face. She was very pale and though she held her head high he fancied that there was a look of fear in her eyes.

"What happened when you put Her Ladyship to bed?" Lord Rothwyn asked.

"Nothing, M'Lord," Elsie replied defiantly.

Then Henry burst in:

"That's not true, M'Lord, but we meant no harm—I swear we meant no harm!"

"What did you do?" Lord Rothwyn asked.

"It was just . . . the lady, M'Lord," Henry said

"What lady?"

"The lady that has been asking almost every day about Her Ladyship's health."

"She asked you?"

"Yes, M'Lord, she came to the side-door the first time I happened to be on duty there. She asked me about Her Ladyship and gave me half a sovereign. I didn't think there were any harm in it—honest, M'Lord!"

"What happened?" Lord Rothwyn asked.

"She came three times this last week," Henry answered.

"Each time she tipped you?"

"Yes, M'Lord."

"Then what happened?"

"She asked me, M'Lord, if she could talk to one of the maids. She said she was interested in Her Ladyship because she'd known here when she was a child."

"So you took Elsie to her?"

"Not to the carriage, M'Lord."

"Then where?"

"To a house, M'Lord."

"Where was that?"

"In Hill Street, M'Lord."

Lord Rothwyn stiffened. A pattern was beginning to emerge.

"Why did you take Elsie, who seldom if ever waits on Her Ladyship?"

"I didn't think Nurse or Miss Robinson would go, M'Lord."

Lord Rothwyn looked again at Elsie.

Now she was palpably nervous, twisting her fingers together.

"Like Henry, I didn't mean any harm, M'Lord."

"What happened? Tell me exactly. I want to know every word that was said!"

Elsie drew a deep breath.

"She seemed a nice lady, M'Lord. She spoke ever so pleasantly about Her Ladyship."

"What did she ask you?"

There was a moment's pause and then the colour surged into Elsie's face.

"I asked you a question," Lord Rothwyn said harshly, "and I expect an answer!"

Elsie dropped her head and said almost inaudibly:

"She asked me if you and Her Ladyship slept in the same room."

"What did you answer?"

"I said no, M'Lord."

"What did the lady reply to that?"

"She said to the gentleman: 'That's what I told you.'"

"Gentleman? What gentleman?" Lord Rothwyn asked sharply.

"There was a gentleman with her in the room, M'Lord."

"What was he like?"

"He were a foreigner, M'Lord."

"Describe him!"

"Rather flashy, M'Lord. He wore a lot of jewellery."

"Was he old or young?"

"Not very young, M'Lord."

"What was his reply to the lady's remark?"

Again there was silence, but this time it appeared that Elsie was really trying to remember what had been said.

"I'm not quite certain I've got it right, M'Lord," she said, "but I think he said, though it didn't make sense to me: 'That makes the merchandise more valuable.' "

Lord Rothwyn drew in his breath sharply.

"What happened after that?" he asked. "I want the truth."

"The lady said there was someone who was very anxious to speak with Her Ladyship, but she'd have to meet him in secret. . . I . . . I . . . thought . . . it was the gentleman in the room."

"What then?" Lord Rothwyn asked.

"She promised me five pounds, M'Lord, if I would arrange for Her Ladyship to come out just for a second to speak to the gentleman who'd be waiting for her in a carriage. I never thought they'd take her away! I never dreamt they'd do such a thing!"

"But you did not usually wait on Her Ladyship."

"The lady gave me some powder to put in the pie for supper. She said it wouldn't harm Nurse or the other house-maids."

"And it was her idea that you should ask her Ladyship to come and find Royal?" Lord Rothwyn asked in a hard voice.

"She told me to say there'd been an accident, M'Lord."

"And what was Henry to receive?" Lord Rothwyn enquired.

"Five pounds, M'Lord," Henry muttered.

Lord Rothwyn was silent for a second and then he said:

"Did they say anything else, either the lady or the gentleman who was with her? Did they say anything—anything except to tell you what to do? Think now, it might be important."

Elsie looked at Henry but he was staring down at his feet. Then she said:

"Just as I was leaving the room, M'Lord, I thought the gentleman said something. I couldn't quite catch it, but it sounded like 'tide.' "

Lord Rothwyn gave an exclamation. Then without another word he pushed passed the servants who were standing in front of the door and ran down the front stairs.

Royal followed Lord Rothwyn before anyone could prevent him.

A footman gave him his hat and cloak, then opened the front door. Outside, a carriage was waiting.

Lord Rothwyn stepped into it.

"To the docks with all possible speed!" he said to the coach-man.

Only as the carriage-door shut and the horses started off did he realise that Royal was sitting beside him on the back seat.

It seemed to Lalitha that she was being carried a long way from Rothwyn House.

She was too frightened to move even when she was thrown from side to side by the movement of the carriage.

The rope was biting into her ankles and she was finding it hard to breathe beneath the heavy thickness of the cloth which covered her face.

She tried to think but her head felt as if it was filled with wool and she was only aware of a fear flickering within her like the pointed tongue of a serpent.

Where was she being taken?

She thought then that she had been right in knowing who had kidnapped her.

She was to be shipped abroad and sold to the highest bidder in some foreign town.

She was too innocent and too unsophisticated to realise exactly what would happen once she was put up for sale, and yet she knew that it would be a degradation and horror beyond anything she could imagine.

What was more, no-one would ever find her and she would never see Lord Rothwyn again.

She found herself thinking how little she would have to remember; his kiss when he had thought she was Sophie, the feel of his head against her breast, and the silk of his hair touching her lips.

Would that be enough to sustain her, to keep her

sane through the terror of what was waiting for her?

She wondered whether there would be any chance of his finding her even perhaps after she had been sold.

Would he think it worth-while to cross the sea to search for her, or would he never guess where she might have gone?

Perhaps, she thought despairingly, he would think she had run away once again.

Yet how could he think such a thing after the happiness of the dinner they had eaten together, the way in which they had talked, and when he must have known how thrilled she was with the drawings he had given to her.

She thought of the moment at which they had been interrupted.

"Lalitha!" he had said and there had been a note in his voice which vibrated through her whole body.

She remembered how she had said to him:

"You will . . . laugh at me for being . . . sentimental."

"I am not laughing," Lord Rothwyn had replied. "I want to tell you something."

What had he wanted to tell her?

She remembered the look in his eyes, a look which had made her thrill and quiver in a manner which she could not translate into words but which had been very wonderful.

She had felt at that moment a strange excitement well up inside her.

It had been impossible to speak; hard even to breathe.

Her eyes had been held by his, so that she thought that he was telling her wonderful things that she had always longed to know but had never heard expressed.

Perhaps she had been mistaken; perhaps she had simply been blinded by her love for him, which made her see things that were not there and imagine something which had no foundation in fact.

She loved him so desperately that just to be near him was to feel herself vibrate to a strange music that came from within her very soul.

She recalled then how she had told him that she

looked at a drawing not with her eyes but with her soul.

After she had read him the poem he had asked her whether she thought the lady to whom Lord Hadley had addressed it had called to his heart.

When she had found it difficult to answer him the note in his voice had changed.

What did it all mean?

Or had it indeed meant nothing?

He was so kind, so sympathetic, that perhaps it was only part of his re-construction of her and meant nothing special to him.

Now she would never know the answers to all the questions which had puzzled her.

She was being taken away. She would never see him again! The future would be a hell worse than anything she had suffered from her Step-mother.

She wanted to scream at the thought but knew what would happen to her if she made a sound.

She was back where she had been before, cringing at the thought of being whipped, expecting to receive a blow, certain of making mistakes because she was so afraid.

"Can I never escape from this?" she asked herself.

She thought someone answered cynically: "Only by death!"

Then Lalitha knew that if what she suspected was true, if she was indeed being taken to some foreign place to be humiliated and degraded in a manner she could not at the moment imagine, then she must die.

She wondered if it would be hard to kill herself and how she should do it.

There would obviously not be a pistol within her reach. Perhaps too prisoners were not allowed to possess knives.

How then could she die?

She felt that if one was determined enough it would not be impossible. Somehow she would find a way, but only when she was certain that Lord Rothwyn would not come to her rescue.

What would he feel if he followed her and then found that she was dead?

Then mockingly the thought came to her that perhaps he would be relieved. She would no longer be an encumbrance upon him, no longer a trouble as she had been up to now.

Why should he concern himself with anyone so tiresome?

She remembered that she did not yet know what he had said to Sophie.

Why had he left Sophie at Roth Park and come in search of her?

Sophie had been so insistent that all he wanted was her love, and that once she had given it to him he would no longer have a thought for anyone else.

But he had left Sophie and followed after her so quickly that he had caught up with the stage-coach before it reached London.

If she had gone on to Norfolk as she had intended, Lalitha thought, it might have been more difficult for him to find her.

He did not know where her Nurse lived.

As far as she knew, he had no idea where her home was before her Step-mother had sold it and they had come to London.

But even if she had managed to change coaches in London and start off for Norwich, Lalitha thought now, that would not have deterred him.

He had not finished with her after all and therefore he would have pursued her as he would pursue her now.

Quite suddenly it seemed to her that there was a light at the end of a very long tunnel.

There·was hope!

There was an irresistible belief deep down within her that he would not let her go. He would find her somehow.

But how would he ever know what had happened?

It had all been so cleverly done, she thought; Nattie and the house-maids ill, Elsie attending her, and because she thought Royal was involved in an accident she had run impetuously from her bed-room so that no-one would know where she had gone.

Lord Rothwyn would be asleep now, confident that she too was sleeping in the next room.

How often had she looked at the communicating door which lay between them?

When he had been ill she had visualised herself opening it and going into him even though he had not asked for her.

He would have been shocked at her presumption, perhaps angry because he would consider it an impertinence.

Yet she would have seen him; she would have heard his voice. Even to listen to him when he was angry with her was better than not hearing him at all.

What would happen when the morning came? Who would tell him that she had not slept in her bed?

Nattie would do so if she was well enough, or would it be Elsie who would keep the house-hold from realising that she was not in the house?

Part of the next day might pass before anybody realised that she was not there, and by that time where would she be?

Lalitha wanted to cry out at the hopelessness of it.

The horses came to a stand-still and she realised that for quite some time they had been rumbling over heavy cobbles which shook the carriage and were very unlike the smooth roads in the smarter part of London.

Now she heard a ship's bell and she was sure that they were down by the river.

For the first time since they had left Park Lane the man beside her spoke.

"Keep quiet an' don't move!" he said. "One sound an' Oi'll sock ye!"

Lalitha heard him open the carriage-door and step outside.

She could hear him talking to another man, but the cloth which covered her head was so thick that it was difficult to distinguish what they said.

Rough hands then picked her up and carried her from the carriage.

There were two men, she knew that.

They placed her on what seemed to be a stretcher

and someone else, a third man, threw some heavy covering over her and pulled it over her feet.

It covered her completely so that now she could hardly breathe.

They were moving and there was a man walking in front and one behind her.

They walked across cobbles and then Lalitha knew that they were taking her up a gangway.

A man spoke to them and although he spoke in English it was with a pronounced foreign accent.

"Down below!" he said. "There's only one more to come, then we sail."

She had been right in what she feared!

She was in a ship and they were taking her across the Channel.

Frantically she began to pray that Lord Rothwyn would somehow find her.

"Save me! Save me!" she called him with her heart. "Find out where they are . . . taking me. Save me because . . . otherwise . . . I must die!"

The men carrying her had set the stretcher down on the deck and now one of them picked her up in his arms and put her over his shoulder.

Her head was hanging down his back and his arm encircled her legs.

He was climbing down a steep companion-way to what appeared to be the bowels of the ship.

He moved along a passage so narrow that his shoulders brushed against the sides.

He unlocked a door, and to enter what Lalitha imagined was a cabin he had to bend his head and he put his other hand on her back so that she would not fall off his shoulder.

Then he set her abruptly down on the floor, so roughly that it hurt.

She gave a little exclamation of pain and then was afraid in case he would be angered by it.

She felt his hands fumbling with the rope tied round her waist, then he pulled the cloth from her head.

For a moment she could see nothing and thought that they had blinded her.

Without speaking he tightened the rope round her hands again, then drew a handkerchief from his pocket and tied it over her mouth.

"This is t' help ye keep silent," he said. "Oi told ye before what'd happen if ye make a noise and that goes for the rest of ye!" he added in a louder tone.

The handkerchief hurt Lalitha's mouth and she suspected that it was not particularly clean.

As the man went from the room, his feet heavy on the bare boards, she realised that there was a faint light coming through one port-hole and that the reason it was hard to see was that it was still dark outside.

The man who had gagged her slammed the door behind him and she heard the key turn in the lock.

She tried to discern to whom he had spoken and who else was in the cabin.

It was very small, low-ceiling, and devoid of any furniture, but gradually as her eyes grew accustomed to the darkness she could distinguish what appeared to be bundles lying on the floor.

Then she knew that, like her, other women were lying there, gagged and bound just as she was.

Gradually the light from the port-hole grew stronger as the faint shimmer of dawn began to dispel the darkness of the night.

Edging herself backwards inch by inch, she sat up and propped herself against a wall.

Now she could see who else was in the cabin.

There were eight other bodies, and as the light increased second by second she could see that they all had frightened eyes above their silenced mouths, and their arms were tied as were their ankles.

'Nine women,' Lalitha thought, 'and one more to come!'

Even as she thought of it she heard heavy foot-steps coming down the passage.

The door was unlocked and the man came into the cabin carrying another woman's body over his shoulder.

He threw her down at the other side of the cabin, pulled the cloth from over her head, tightened the rope round her waist, and gagged her.

She was a very young pretty girl with fair, golden hair, and although she gave a little whimper before the gag was applied she was obviously too frightened to make any noise.

"We be a-sailing now," the man said, "an' when we be out at sea ye'll be untied if ye behave yeselves. Oi expect anyhow ye'll want t' be sick!"

He laughed as if at a joke, then went from the cabin, locking the door behind him.

Overhead was the sound of hurrying feet and the slap of sails being set.

'We are leaving England,' Lalitha thought. 'I am being carried over the sea and no-one will ever know what has happened to me.'

She wondered if it would be possible to free herself and make one wild dash to the Quay.

Then she realised that even if it were possible to undo the cords which bound her, there was a locked door to prevent her escape and the only port-hole in the cabin faced out onto the river.

Lalitha also knew only too well the kind of punishment she would incur for trying to run away.

She was certain that the man had not spoken idly when he had said he would knock her senseless.

Looking round the cabin, Lalitha saw that two of the girls were lying with closed eyes and appeared to be asleep.

She was certain that if they were sleeping it was not a natural slumber.

The others were all staring round as she was; their eyes wide, their pupils dilated with fear.

Lalitha realised that the majority of the girls were just as Lord Rothwyn had described to her—from the country.

There was no mistaking the freshness about them or the fact that they were very young, perhaps fifteen or sixteen at the most.

She could see that they wore solid, hard-wearing country boots, the type purchased by domestic servants, beneath home-made dresses of cotton or coarse wool.

What was to be their fate—and what hers?

She heard the anchor being wound up and mooring-ropes cast off. Then there were voices shouting orders and the movement of the ship became more obvious as the wind filled the sails.

It was very cold and Lalitha shivered in her thin evening-gown.

They must have now turned from the Quay and into the centre of the river. There was a glimmer of sunshine coming through the dirty port-hole.

Lalitha wondered if it was shining into Lord Rothwyn's bed-room and whether it would awaken him.

Still her heart was calling to him and she wondered if he would realise how desperately she needed him.

He was so strong, also so perceptive.

Was it possible to reach him, mentally if not physically?

Always she had believed in the power of thought; always she had been convinced that the mind knew no limits, no boundaries.

But would such ideas work in practice when the moment came for them to prove themselves?

'Come to . . . me! I want . . . you! I need . . . you! Save . . . me!'

She sent out her cry again and again and with it a prayer.

'Please, God . . . let him . . . hear me . . . let him know I am in danger . . . Make him understand . . . please, God . . . please, God. . . .'

Then she knew that it was hopeless! The ship was moving with the tide, which was carrying her away from London and downriver to the sea.

Her cry, like her prayers, had failed!

Lord Rothwyn had not heard and now there was no hope for either herself or the other wretched girls beside her.

The girl sitting next to Lalitha, whom she had not noticed before, managed to slip the gag from her mouth and it fell over her chin to her chest.

"What's happening? Where are we going?" she asked in a frightened voice.

She had a country accent and Lalitha, turning her head to look at her, saw that she was pretty in a child-like, somewhat bovine manner.

She was plump and healthy-looking with rosy apple cheeks, if she had not been pale with fright.

Because the girl had managed to free herself of the gag Lalitha moved her lips against the dirty handkerchief which covered her mouth and it slipped to her chin.

The girl who had been watching her said before she could speak:

"That's better! 'Tis a bit frightening talking to one-self!"

"I know!" Lalitha answered.

"What's a-going on?" the girl asked. "I dinna understand what's happening."

"Where do you come from?" Lalitha enquired.

"I come from Somerset," the girl replied. "I'd a position promised me in London."

"What sort of position?"

"Kitchen-maid to a Nobleman," the girl replied.

Her face puckered for a moment as she said:

"I tells her where she was to take me."

"Who did you tell?" Lalitha enquired.

"The woman who met me at the Coaching-Inn. 'Where do you want to go?' she asked. When I told her she said she'd drive me there. She had a nice carriage and I thought I might as well go comfortable like instead of walking."

"What happened then?" Lalitha asked.

"I don't rightly know," the girl answered. "She says to me: 'You must be tired after your journey. Here's a drink for you.' But after I had drunk it I felt all funny like, and I didn't know anything until I found myself here tied up. What's the game? What are they a-doing?"

Lalitha was silent. There seemed no point in upsetting this child unduly.

"I expect they will tell us sooner or later," she said, "but I am afraid we have been kidnapped."

"Kidnapped?" the girl exclaimed, "and what would

be the point of that? I ain't got more than 5 pence on me."

Lalitha did not answer.

She could only feel afraid and knew that making the others feel equally afraid would not help.

She looked at the other girls and realised that they were trying, as she had done, to remove the gags, but either they were not so clever at it or else the gags had been more tightly tied, for they were unable to free themeslves.

The girl from Somerset began to cry.

"I wants to go home to me mother!" she sobbed. "I thought t'wood be fine to be in London, to be able to send money home to th' family, but I'm frightened! I wants to go home!"

"That is what we all want," Lalitha longed to reply.

Instead she said quietly:

"You must be brave. It will be no help to annoy these people who have kidnapped us. They might be rough or unkind if they thought we did not obey them."

"You mean they'd . . . hurt us?" the girl asked.

Lalitha drew in her breath.

She remembered Lord Rothwyn saying that the "White Slave Traders" would beat or drug those who did not do as they were told.

'God help us all!' she thought.

She knew despairingly that the ship was gathering impetus and they were moving quicker than they had before.

There was a strong wind, and she reckoned that if it continued they would not take many hours to cross the Channel to Holland or wherever they were going.

They would be there before evening, and what would await them?

She looked at the other girls and realised that she must be the oldest present.

There was no reason, she thought, for her to be included in this human cargo if the Slavers had not been coerced or paid.

She knew then as if someone had told her it was her Step-mother who had arranged it all.

Perhaps Sophie had gone back from Roth Park to say that instead of attending to her as she had expected him to do, Lord Rothwyn had chased after the stage-coach.

Lalitha could imagine her Step-mother's fury if she believed that Sophie with all her beauty had lost such a fine matrimonial catch as Lord Rothwyn.

She doubted, despite what Sophie had said, that Julius Verton was still at her feet.

If he had been, Lalitha was quite certain that, rather than take the trouble to destroy the evidence of her marriage to Lord Rothwyn, Sophie would have contented herself with the man to whom she was already engaged.

Thinking back over the events of that night it was obvious that Julius Verton had received the note the groom had carried to him at Wimbledon.

He was a rather stupid, immature young man.

At the same time he had his pride, and while he might have been broken-hearted at losing Sophie, his blue-blood would have ensured that he would not crawl back to plead for her favours after she had jilted him so heartlessly.

Besides, he would have been fortified in his resolution by his grandmother and his friends.

Lalitha was sure that Sophie's note would have made it clear that she had finished with him.

Despite her beauty, the marriage from the point of view of a very elegible young man who would inherit a Dukedom was a *mésalliance*.

His relatives would have expected him to do far better.

There was no doubt that he would have been welcomed by most match-making Mamas.

Lalitha was certain now that Sophie had tried to entice back Lord Rothwyn because Julius Verton was no longer available. If she lost him then the only suitor left who had offered her marriage was the dissolute, aged, and unpleasant Sir Thomas Whernside.

'No wonder neither she nor her mother will ever forgive me!' Lalitha thought humbly.

And yet despite his chivalrous action in stopping the

stage-coach and being ready to take her back to Roth Park, Lord Rothwyn might still have a tenderness for Sophie.

How could he resist anyone so beautiful, so alluring, that other women paled into insignificance beside her?

'How could I ever expect him to care for me?' Lalitha wondered miserably.

Her thoughts had carried her away from the desperateness of her situation and she was jerked back to reality when the girl from Somerset asked with a break in her voice:

"Can't we do anything? Can't we escape from here?"

"I cannot think how," Lalitha answered. "Can you undo the cords round your waist?"

"Not on my own," the girl answered, "but I might try and undo yours."

"How could you do that?" Lalitha asked.

"If we sat back to back," she answered.

"How clever of you!" Lalitha exclaimed. "I never thought of that!"

They pushed themselves round with their heels until they were sitting with their backs against each other. Then Lalitha felt the girl's fingers working at the cords which bound her round the waist.

It took some time, but finally Lalitha managed to squeeze her hands free, then hastily she turned to undo the girl from Somerset.

"They said they would unfasten us when we are out to sea," she said. "When they come back we had best pretend we are still tied or we might be in trouble!"

"I understand," the girl said. "What about the others?"

"I think we could loosen their gags," Lalitha said. "What we must do is to let them down as far as their chins so that they can quickly edge them up over their mouths again."

She saw that the girls had understood this and, propelling herself with her bound feet, she moved round one side of the cabin while the girl from Somerset moved to the other to loosen the gags.

The girls all seemed bewildered as to what had happened.

"Where are we going?" "Where be they a-taking us?" "What do they want?" "I'm frightened!"

The same sentences came out one after another, mostly spoken with country accents although there were one or two cockneys amongst them.

When Lalitha reached the two girls who were insensible, she found them both sleeping so heavily that she guessed they were drugged.

They must have drunk a stronger dose than the girl from Somerset had been given.

They were both pretty girls, very young, both fair-haired with strong, well-formed bodies already with the promise of maturity.

'Perhaps they are happier as they are,' Lalitha thought. 'At least they do not know what lies ahead of them.'

"Keep your voices low," she said to the other girls as they bewailed their fate, while two or three of them wept bitterly and kept crying for their mothers.

The noise overheard continued or rather it seemed to intensify as Lalitha guessed that the ship was moving into stronger waters.

Certainly the river was more turbulent and waves began to slap against the sides.

It was then that she heard men shouting and she thought that there was a note of alarm in their tones.

Some of them were speaking a foreign language, so it might have been her imagination, but it was impossible for her to hear distinctly.

Then unexpectedly there was the sound of heavy foot-steps running along the passageway outside the cabin.

Quickly Lalitha and the girl from Somerset pushed up their gags and slipped their hands through the rope which was wound round their bodies. But not before Lalitha had hissed in a low voice to the others:

"Put on your gags!"

Her own was rather loose and she kept her head bent.

Four men burst into the cabin, crossed it, and started to pull at the rough wooden wall opposite the door.

To Lalitha's astonishment one long panel about three foot wide slid away and behind it was a dark cavity.

The men bent down to pick up the girls from the floor.

But the man who had brought Lalitha aboard, who appeared to be in authority, said:

"Tighten their gags! Us dinna want them trying to call out!"

The man forced Lalitha's teeth open with the handkerchief and tied it so tightly that it was very painful.

One girl gave a scream of pain and received a blow on the side of her head which knocked her half unconscious.

Unfortunately as a man lifted the girl from Somerset the cord round her waist trailed loose.

"Blast th' little bitch," the man exclaimed. "Her's gone and loosened 'erself!"

"Tie 'er up again, 'er'll be punished later," came the order. "An' see th' others can't move."

Lalitha's cord was tightened over her waist and the men started to heave the girls through the opening in the cabin's wall into the darkness beyond.

Two men swung Lalitha through the opening and she found herself lying on rough wooden struts and knew that they were hidden in what was just a space at the stern of the ship for which there was no other use.

It was without light and there was very little air and the girls were tumbled one on top of the other.

When the last one was deposited the man who had brought Lalitha aboard said:

"One squeak out o' any o' ye and Oi'll kill ye! Do ye understand? Ye'll die!"

As he spoke he stepped back into the cabin and the piece of wall was replaced.

It fitted exactly, in fact there was not even a chink of light to show where it had been.

There was no doubt that the sails were being lowered. Although Lalitha was not certain, she fancied that she could hear the sound of another vessel coming alongside.

Men were shouting at each other but again she could not understand what was being said.

She lay shivering with cold and fear and knew that the girls round her were all trembling.

After a long time when she had begun to think that she had been mistaken and there must be other reasons why the ship should have lowered sail, there was the sound of foot-steps and voices coming down the passage.

The door was opend and with a sudden leap of her heart so that she seemed almost to suffocate, Lalitha heard Lord Rothwyn's voice:

"What is in here?" he asked.

"Just an empty cabin, Sir. All th' cargo, as ye've seen, 'as been stowed amid ships."

Lalitha struggled frantically against her gag but it was tight. She would have drummed with her feet on the flooring but they were resting on the body of another girl.

'He . . . will . . . see and . . . hear . . . nothing!' she thought despairingly, and cried out in her heart:

'Save . . . me . . . I am . . . here . . . save me!'

There was a sudden whining and scraping against the cabin-wall behind which she was hidden.

It was Royal!

Lalitha knew the sounds he made when he was excited and when he was trying to get to her.

Then she heard Lord Rothwyn say:

"I wonder what is arousing my dog? He seems to sense there must be something behind that wall."

"Rats, Sir!" the man exclaimed, "the ship be riddled with 'em. You have a sporting little beast there."

"Strange that he should be so excited," Lord Rothwyn said.

Then he raised his voice.

"Officer," he called, "there is something here I would like to show you."

"There be nothin'!" the man insisted. "Nothin' at all! Ye be wasting yer time, Sir."

"I trust my dog's instinct," Lord Rothwyn answered coldly.

There was the sound of two more men approaching and a quiet voice said:

"You wanted me, M'Lord?"

"Yes," Lord Rothwyn answered. "I think my dog has found something."

It was then that Lalitha, with a super-human effort which scraped away the skin, freed her hands.

Pulling the gag from her mouth, she tried to scream. Although it was not a loud noise it was still a sound.

Then even as the Revenue Officers opened up the wall Royal jumped into the darkness, yapping with excitement, to lick her face.

She was lifted into the cabin and while her ankles were still tied she was standing upright and Lord Rothwyn had his arms round her.

"Y-you . . . have . . . come!" she cried incoherently, hiding her face against his shoulder. "I . . . knew . . . I was sure . . . you would . . . hear me . . . calling . . . you."

Chapter Eight

Lalitha gave a semi-conscious little cry of fear, then awoke to find that she was in her own bed at Rothwyn House.

Although the curtains were drawn she could see the dim outline of the white and gold walls, the cupids over the mirror on the dressing-table, and the huge vases of lilies and roses which scented the room.

She was safe! She was home and she need no longer be afraid!

It was hard to remember what had happened since the moment she had found herself held closely in Lord Rothwyn's arms and she knew that the horror of being carried away from England was over.

Someone had untied the cord from round her ankles,

and then Lord Rothwyn had taken his cape from his
shoulders and covered her with it.

He had helped her along the narrow passage and
up onto the deck of the ship.

She remembered seeing Revenue Officers with pistols
in their hands lining up the sailors who manned the
ship, but Lord Rothwyn had hurried her to where
she must climb down a rope-ladder and into a small
boat.

There was a large Revenue Cutter floating alongside
the ship in which she had been abducted and she
could see that there were many more men drawn up
on deck, all fully armed, so that there could be no
question of their being opposed by any sort of violence.

She was too bemused by what had happened to think
of anything except that Lord Rothwyn was beside her
and she need no longer be afraid that she would never
see him again.

They were rowed the short distance to a Quay a long
way down-river from where they had embarked, but
nevertheless there waiting for them was the carriage.

Lord Rothwyn helped Lalitha inside and Royal
jumped in to nestle against her, his head in her lap.

It was perhaps the little dog's demonstration of his
affection as she stroked his head which broke the control Lalitha was keeping over herself ever since she
had been saved.

Without really thinking about it she turned towards
Lord Rothwyn, hid her face against his shoulder, and
the tears came.

He held her close as the horses started off and after
a short silence he said gently:

"It is all right! It is all over!"

"I . . . knew you would . . . save me," she whispered.
"I c-called and called for . . . you with my . . . heart
. . . like the poem."

Her voice was muffled and indistinct with tears and
Lord Rothwyn's arms tightened round her as he replied:

"I heard you call. It awakened me, but the credit for
saving you must go to Royal."

"Would you . . . have . . . gone away," she asked,
"if he had not . . . scratched at the . . . wall?"

"I had every intention of tearing the ship apart," he answered, "because Royal was so certain you were there."

Lalitha's tears were checked by her curiosity as he went on:

"When I reached the Quay there were a number of ships tied up alongside it and I walked along seeking which one was likely to sail on the morning tide. Then when we came to an empty berth Royal showed me that you had been there."

"How did he do . . . that?" Lalitha asked.

"He ran about wildly sniffing the ground and making it very clear that this was where you had been. I had a Revenue Officer with me because I had already explained to him what I suspected might have happened."

"Why did you . . . suspect?" Lalitha asked.

"I will tell you that later," Lord Rothwyn replied. "At the moment I am explaining about Royal."

"Yes . . . of course," she murmured.

" 'What ship has recently left here?' I enquired, and the Revenue Officer asked the same question of some dockers."

"They told him it was a Dutch ship already moving down the river but still in sight.

" 'What was her cargo?' the Revenue Officer asked.

" 'Corpses for one thing!' one of the men replied and laughed."

Lord Rothwyn paused.

"It was then we set off in the Revenue Cutter after your ship."

"I thought I . . . should never . . . see . . . you again," Lalitha said, and now the tears were pouring down her cheeks.

She thought, that Lord Rothwyn was about to say something, but he checked himself. He just held her close against him until she stopped crying, and then he gave her his handkerchief to wipe her eyes.

When they arrived at Rothwyn House it was still very early in the morning, but half the house-hold seemed to be waiting for their arrival.

Nattie was there, looking a little pale but otherwise she was her usual self.

Lord Rothwyn helped Lalitha into the Hall; then, as he realised that she was feeling too weak to climb the stairs, he picked her up in his arms.

She weighed no more than a child and he carried her up the staircase to her bed-room and set her down gently on the bed.

"Look after her, Nattie," he said in his deep voice. "Her Ladyship is exhausted. What she needs is sleep."

He would have left Lalitha, but her hands went out to hold on to him and she said in a whisper:

"Are you . . . going . . . away?"

"I have to leave you for a little while," he answered, "but I promise that you will be well protected. No-one will be allowed into this room without Nattie's permission, and there will be two of my most trusted men on guard outside it, not because there is anything more to fear, but only that you should not feel insecure."

He looked down into her eyes, and seeing that she was still uncertain he said with a smile:

"Trust me! I promise that I will never lose you again!"

He saw a sudden light come into her eyes, as if the words had a special meaning for her. Then he was gone from the room and Nattie put her to bed.

She had been given a drink, Lalitha remembered, which tasted of honey and herbs and she knew now that it must have made her sleep deep and dreamlessly until this moment.

It must be getting on in the day, she thought, then heard the clock in the Hall chime and count the strokes:

"Five . . . six . . . seven . . . it could not be!"

She stirred, then realised that Nattie was sitting in the room in an arm-chair by the fire-place.

She rose and came across to the bed.

"You're awake, M'Lady?"

"Is it really seven o'clock?" Lalitha asked.

"You've had a good sleep. Things'll seem better now. I'll order you something to eat."

Nattie rang the bell.

"Might I not dine with . . . His Lordship?" Lalitha asked.

"His Lordship has not yet returned."

"Not . . . returned?"

Lalitha sat up in bed.

"Why? Where has he gone?"

Then before Nattie could reply she knew the answer to the question.

He would have been seeing about the girls who, like herself, had been kidnapped.

He would, she felt, feel it his duty to do what he could for them, just as he would also see that the "White Slave Traders" be brought to justice.

When the food came—delicious, beautifully cooked dishes to tempt the appetite—Lalitha managed to sample a number of them because she knew that it would please Nattie.

At the same time she was not really hungry.

All she wanted was to see Lord Rothwyn, to find out what had happened, above all to know that he was there and that the future need not hold any terrors for her.

She wished now that she had told him she was certain it was her Step-mother who had contrived her capture.

She wanted to ask Nattie questions about Elsie and Henry, but somehow she felt uncomfortable at discussing anything that had occurred until Lord Rothwyn returned.

She had the feeling that he would not wish her to do so.

After she had finished her dinner Lalitha found that she was no longer tired, and the exhaustion she had felt when Lord Rothwyn had brought her back from the ship had gone completely.

Her deep sleep and perhaps the healing herbs, which she was sure had come from the Herb-Woman, swept away all the physical ill-effects arising from her experience, but she knew that there were others which only Lord Rothwyn could alleviate.

Time passed and Nattie insisted on getting her ready for bed.

She brushed her hair until it shone, brought her a fresh night-gown, and Royal was collected for his evening walk.

"Who is taking him out?" Lalitha asked apprehensively.

"Mr. Hobson himself!" Nattie replied.

Lalitha could not help a little smile to think that the Major-Domo should condescend to perform a task which was usually allotted to one of the junior footmen.

When Royal's return was heralded by a knock at the door Lalitha heard Nattie speaking for a moment to the Major-Domo outside.

She came back into the room not only with Royal but she carried a large crested silver ice-bucket in which reposed a bottle of champagne.

"His Lordship has returned!" she announced.

"He is . . . back!" Lalitha exclaimed.

"He will join Your Ladyship after he has bathed and changed," Nattie answered.

Lalitha drew in a deep breath.

Somehow it was impossible to speak.

She could only feel as if every nerve in her body had come to life and that she had been waiting a century for this moment.

Nattie set the champagne down on a small table beside a wing-back arm-chair. Then she fetched from the Major-Domo, who was still outside the door, a silver salver on which reposed two cut-crystal glasses.

"I'll leave you now, M'Lady," Nattie said. "Is there anything else you require?"

"No, nothing, thank you," Lalitha answered. "I am so grateful, Nattie, that you stayed with me all today. It must have been very boring for you."

"I had plenty to do saying prayers of thankfulness for Your Ladyship's safe return," Nattie answered.

She spoke with a throb in her voice, and Lalitha thought that there was a suspicion of tears in her old eyes as she turned away abruptly.

'Can she really be so fond of me?' she wondered humbly, and was deeply grateful that anyone could care for her so much.

As soon as the door had closed behind Nattie, Royal

jumped up onto the bed as he knew he was not supposed to do.

He made a fuss of Lalitha and she had the feeling that he too was waiting for the appearance of his Master.

They waited for what seemed a long time. Then Royal began to wag his tail and there was a knock at the communicating door. Without waiting for an answer it opened.

Lord Rothwyn came into the room and Lalitha felt as if it were lit by a hundred candles.

He was not dressed as she had expected, but was wearing a long silk robe in which she had never seen him before.

He closed the door behind him and walked slowly across the room to where she sat up under the carved canopy against the lace-trimmed pillows, her hair falling over her shoulders.

She looked very frail and insubstantial, and yet beneath the thin material of her night-gown he could see the soft curves of her breasts.

Her eyes were very large and seemed to fill her whole face. There was a light in them that he had never seen before.

"You are all right?" he asked.

"You must be very tired," she answered. "Is your wound aching? You have not done too much?"

"Are you really worrying about me, Lalitha?" he enquired.

"But of course I am worrying," she answered. "You should have taken things very easy your first day out."

Lord Rothwyn smiled and then he said:

"I think in the circumstances I might prescribe for us both a glass of champagne!"

"It is there!" Lalitha said, indicating the silver wine-cooler with her hand.

Lord Rothwyn drew the bottle from the ice which encircled it and poured some of the golden liquid into each of the crystal glasses.

He carried one to Lalitha, picked up the other for himself, and said:

"We must celebrate the fact that we are together again."

There was something in his tone which made her drop her eyes before his.

"Shall we drink to our happiness?"

"I would . . . like to do . . . that," she answered almost in a whisper.

Lord Rothwyn raised his glass.

"May we be happy ever after!" he said very softly and drank.

Lalitha sipped the champagne and felt as if it were sun-shine running through her.

A little shyly because standing by the bed Lord Rothwyn seemed so tall and over-powering she said:

"You should sit down. There is so much I want to ask you, but I do not wish to be a nuisance if you are tired."

Lord Rothwyn re-filled his glass before he replied:

"I do not admit to feeling tired, but as we have a lot to say to each other I am quite prepared to make myself as comfortable as possible. Shall we sit close together as we did that night in the hut?"

Lalitha's eyes went to his wonderingly.

Without waiting for her permission he sat down on the bed beside her with his back against the pillows, his legs stretched out in front of him on the satin and lace covers.

Lalitha felt a little quiver of excitement go through her because he was so near.

He had held her in his arms when they had driven back together from the ship, but she had been too distressed, too bewildered, to think of anything except that she was safe.

Now she was vividly conscious of him and of her love, so that it was difficult to repress an impulse to hide her face once again against his shoulder.

"Where shall we begin?" Lord Rothwyn asked.

"Tell me how you found me," Lalitha begged.

"I awoke at two o'clock with the feeling that you had called me."

"Then you did hear me!" she exclaimed with a little cry of excitement. "I was sure that you would hear me crying out in my heart . . . for . . . you to . . . save me!"

"When I was awake," Lord Rothwyn went on, "I heard Royal whining."

He went on to tell her how he had discovered that both Henry and Elsie had been questioned by her Step-mother.

At the mere mention of the woman who had terrorised her for so long he felt Lalitha tremble beside him.

"I was . . . sure it was . . . she!" she said. "I knew she would never . . . forgive me because you had not . . . stayed with Sophie when she came to Roth Park. She will never . . . rest until she . . . destroys me!"

"That is something she will never do!" Lord Rothwyn said.

"But she has . . . tried and will go on . . . trying," Lalitha murmured unhappiily.

"After I had assisted the Revenue Officers to charge not only the Captain of the ship for kidnapping you and those unfortunate girls who were with you," Lord Rothwyn went on, "they took into custody the man who owned the ship and two others like him. He is undoubtedly the head of an organisation that has been operating for some time."

"You caught him!" Lalitha said. "Oh, I am glad of that!"

"When he was disposed of," Lord Rothwyn went on, "and those young girls had been sent back to their families, I called on Mrs. Clements on Hill Street."

"Mrs. C-Clements?" Lalitha faltered.

"She was never married to your father," Lord Rothwyn said. "I have been carrying on an investigation for some time, not from anything you have told me directly because I knew you were afraid of what would happen if you did. But from information you let drop inadvertently I pieced together a very clear picture of what had happened."

"You . . . guessed that she had . . . taken Mama's . . . place?" Lalitha whispered beneath her breath.

"I found out exactly what she had done," Lord

Rothwyn said, "and how she had pretended that Sophie was your father's legitimate daughter and foisted her upon Society."

He felt Lalitha shiver and he said quickly:

"You need never be afraid of her again. She is dead!"

"Dead?" Lalitha gasped.

"I confronted her with the information that there was a warrant out for her arrest," Lord Rothwyn said. "There was a charge of swindling, for which the penalty is transportation, and another for the kidnapping and exploitation of a minor for immoral purposes, for which the penalty is death!"

He paused before he went on:

"However, since your name would inevitably have been involved in the proceedings, I gave Mrs. Clements a chance of escape before the police arrived. There was a ship sailing to New South Wales at noon today and I told her that if she was travelling on it the warrant could only be put into execution if she ever returned to this country."

"She . . . agreed?" Lalitha asked incredibly.

"She had no choice," Lord Rothwyn said, and she realised by the tone of his voice how fierce and ruthless he had been.

"I escorted her to the Quay," he went on. "The ship was standing out in the river ready to sail and the last passengers to go aboard were taken off in a row-boat, Mrs. Clements among them.

"I watched her go," he continued, "to ensure that there was no trickery at the last moment. Then even as the boat reached the side of the ship and the rope-ladders were being let down for the passengers, she threw herself into the river.

Lalitha gave a little gasp.

"The tide was running very swiftly. I imagine, from what I saw, that she could not swim, nor, I suspect, could any of the men manning the boat."

"She . . . drowned!" Lalitha whispered.

"There was no chance of rescuing her," Lord Rothwyn replied. "She was swept away by the current and before anyone could realise what had happened she disappeared!"

Lalitha found it difficult to get her breath.

Very gently Lord Rothwyn put his arm round her and drew her very close to him.

"The nightmare is over!" he said. "There is no longer any darkness to frighten you."

Lalitha hid her face against his shoulder.

"You are free, Lalitha!" he said, "free of all that has frightened you and made you so miserable these last years. I now know who you are, that your father was respected by all who knew him, and your mother was someone everyone loved."

He felt Lalitha give a little sob and he continued:

"They would both want you to be happy and that is what I am determined you shall be!"

"Sophie! What has . . . happened to . . . Sophie?"

She felt Lord Rothwyn stiffen a little before he replied in a very different tone of voice:

"I thought at first of making Sophie go with her mother. Then, because she once meant something to me, I gave her when she pleaded with me permission to marry Sir Thomas Whernside."

"H-How . . . could . . . she?" Lalitha asked. "He is . . . horrible!"

"She was only too willing to do so," Lord Rothwyn answered. "But Whernside, as he has told me frankly, can no longer afford the extravagances and the luxuries of London. He is therefore taking Sophie with him to his Estate in the North and it is very unlikely that he will ever again be able to afford to come South."

Lalitha was silent for a moment and then she said:

"But you . . . loved her! She is so . . . very . . . beautiful!"

It seemed to her that there was a long silence before Lord Rothwyn said:

"Last night I asked you which you thought the more beautiful—my picture over the mantel-piece or the drawings I brought you—do you remember?"

"Y-Yes . . . of course," Lalitha answered.

"And you told me," Lord Rothwyn went on, "that

the drawings inspired you and you looked at them with
your soul."

"Yes . . . I said . . . that."

"I bought those three particular drawings," Lord
Rothwyn continued, "because each one of them reminded me of you."

"Of . . . me?"

"There is so much in them, so much below the
surface," Lord Rothwyn said. "*The Running Youth*
has all the joy of living which you have now that you
are well again. *The Landscape* is your enthralling,
fascinating mind."

He paused to say slowly:

"The face of the angel by Leonardo da Vinci has
a spiritual, mystical look of which no man could ever
tire."

He felt Lalitha quiver and then she said:

"I do . . . not . . . understand."

"What I am telling you, my darling," he said softly,
"is that you are not only the most beautiful person I
have ever seen in my life, but your beauty enthralls
me, delights and inspires me, and I shall never tire of
looking at you!"

"It . . . cannot be . . . true!" Lalitha said. "Can you
be . . . saying these . . . things to . . . me?"

Lord Rothwyn looked down at her face raised to his
and said very gently:

"Had you not guessed by this time that I love you?"

He saw the sudden radiance which lit her face and
then as she stared at him wide-eyed he went on:

"When I saw how badly you had been treated I
thought what I felt was pity. At the same time I felt
an irresistible urge to restore you to what you should
be, re-construct and re-build you."

His arms tightened as he went on:

"I knew instinctively that beneath the scars and
ravages of what had been inflicted upon you there was
a beauty and a treasure beyond price!"

He drew her still closer as he said:

"You called to me for help, Lalitha, and it was a
call not only from your heart but the call of love!"

"Are you . . . sure?" she stammered. "Are you . . . quite, . . . quite sure? Perhaps I am . . . dreaming."

He smiled at the almost childish terror in her voice.

"You are not dreaming," he answered, "but I have been so afraid of telling you this, my precious, in case I should frighten you more than you were frightened already. But I love you! And I cannot risk losing you for the third time!"

Lalitha looked into his eyes and saw that what he said was the truth.

With a little inarticulate cry she hid her face once again.

"The only way I can make sure of you," Lord Rothwyn went on, "is that you should be with me always and at all times, by day and by—night, Lalitha, as my wife."

She did not answer but he could feel her heart beating tempestuously against his through the silk of his robe.

Very gently he put his fingers under her chin and turned her face up to his.

"I love you, my darling!" he said softly. "And now tell me what you feel for me?"

Just for a moment it was impossible to speak, then Lalitha answered.

"I love . . . you! I have loved you . . . I think . . . since you first . . . kissed me . . . but I never . . . thought . . . I never . . . dreamt that I could mean . . . anything to . . . you!"

"I have never forgotten the touch of your lips," Lord Rothwyn said. "They were soft and frightened, but I knew in that moment it was different from any kiss I had ever had before!"

He bent his head towards her and asked softly:

"Shall I discover if it was as wonderful as I remember?"

Her lips were waiting for him and then as his mouth found hers she felt all the wonder and the rapture of her love flare blindingly into something so beautiful, so glorious, that it was like the touch of the Divine.

This was what she had dreamt of but had never believed it could happen to her.

This was an ecstasy beyond imagination, beyond thought itself!

Lord Rothwyn's lips were at first very gentle and yet compelling.

Then as he felt Lalitha respond, as he felt the fire within himself ignite the flame within her so that she quivered against him and he knew that she vibrated to his touch, he became more possessive, more demanding.

He raised his head to look at her face, transfigured by her love into a beauty he had never seen before.

"My precious! My darling!" he said, his voice deep and unsteady. "I will make you happy, I will protect you and look after you and nothing shall ever harm you."

"I love . . . you!" Lalitha murmured. "But you are so . . . wonderful . . . so . . . magnificent! I am . . . afraid of . . . failing you!"

Lord Rothwyn smiled.

"You need not be afraid of that! I need you as I have never needed another woman!"

He saw the question in Lalitha's eyes and went on:

"Women have always wanted something from me in one way or another. Whilst I have been prepared to give them what they demanded, I always felt something was missing. Then the other night when I was with you in the wood-cutters' hut I realised what it was."

"What . . . was it?" Lalitha asked.

"It was the protection that a woman gives a man when she loves him fully and completely, as I believe you love me," he answered.

His voice was very tender as he went on:

"When I awoke to find your arms round me and my head on your breast, I knew that what I had never had from a woman before was the feeling of being encircled with love and that she wanted to keep me safe, although from what I was not quite certain!"

"I was . . . wishing," Lalitha said hesitatingly, "to . . . save you from all that was . . . unpleasant or . . . evil in life. I thought too . . ."

She hesitated and could not look at him.

"Go on," Lord Rothwyn prompted.

. . . that you were . . . almost like my . . . child,"
she whispered, "and I must . . . defend you against . . .
unhappiness and . . . loneliness."

He made a sound that was one of triumph.

"My precious! My lovely one!" he exclaimed. "That
is what I felt you must be thinking. Instinctively in
myself that was what I have always wanted of a woman, without being able to put it into words!"

His lips sought hers and then before he actually
kissed her, Lalitha said softly:

"It was . . . perhaps . . . then that my . . . heart
called to . . . yours."

"The call that I heard," Lord Rothwyn replied, "was
the call of love which will be there all through our
lives."

He kissed her and it seemed to Lalitha that his lips
were more insistent, more demanding, more passionate
than they had been before.

He was asking something of her. Although she was
not certain what it might be, she knew that she was
willing to surrender herself completely and utterly to
whatever he asked.

She was his in mind, body, and soul, and she felt
that he too was giving her himself.

They were one.

They were complete and the call of the heart had
been answered with love.

ABOUT THE AUTHOR

BARBARA CARTLAND, the celebrated romantic author, historian, playwright, lecturer, political speaker and television personality, has now written over 150 books. Miss Cartland has had a number of historical books published and several biographical ones, including that of her brother, Major Ronald Cartland, who was the first Member of Parliament to be killed in the War. This book had a Foreword by Sir Winston Churchill.

In private life, Barbara Cartland, who is a Dame of the Order of St. John of Jerusalem, has fought for better conditions and salaries for Midwives and Nurses. As President of the Royal College of Midwives (Hertfordshire Branch), she has been invested with the first Badge of Office ever given in Great Britain, which was subscribed to by the Midwives themselves. She has also championed the cause for old people and founded the first Romany Gypsy Camp in the world.

Barbara Cartland is deeply interested in Vitamin Therapy and is President of the British National Association for Health.